A Child of Crackhead II

- A Novel Written by –

Shameek A. Speight

A Child of a Crackhead II

ISBN-13:978-1456562366 ISBN-10:1456562363
Email: https://www.createspace.com/3551975

This novel is a work of fiction. Any resemblances to actual events, real people, living or dead, organization, establishments, locales are products of the author's imagination. Other names, characters, places, and incidents are used fictitiously.

Cover design/Graphics:www.mariondesigns.com
Editor: Kelly Klem

Acknowledgments:

It has only been the power of God, my lord and savior Jesus Christ, that I have been able to persevere through many of the trials I've been dealt in my life. I thank him for giving me the strength to move on.

To my beloved sister's, thank you, for believing in me. To my auntie, I love you. To my daughter Niomi, I do all this for you baby.

To Kelly Klem, my best friend, I couldn't have done this without you. To Cierra Waugh, my typist, I couldn't have done this without you. To all the men and women locked up, keep your head up and keep the faith. There will be a brighter day. To Antonie Inch Thomas, what can I say; you taught me the book game and held me down when I was trapped up. I wouldn't know what I know now without you, thank you. To Jilene Carter thank you sweetie, To Charmaine Thomas, Tilla Thomas, Enica Thomas-Smith and my brother Anthony Anglin my other family thank you for the love To all the fans that buy my book, thank you for your love and support.

Chapter 1

Ten years later, the hustlers on the corner watched her voluptuous body walk down the sidewalk with another man. "Damn shorty, your fine as hell," one of the hustlers yelled out not caring who she was with. The man wrapped his arm around her waist and pulled her closer in to him. They continued to walk down the sidewalk and around the block. As soon as they turned the corner and they were out of sight, he let go of her waist and said, "Bitch, didn't I tell you to walk beside me, not in front of me or behind me?" He said as he slapped her so hard across her face that she went flying to the ground.

"But baby, I was walking beside you. I can't help that I have a nice body. The guys are going to look." She said while crying and rubbing her face.

"What? Bitch, you want to talk back?" He bent down and began to punch her furiously in the face, busting her lip and her eyes were swollen shut.

While screaming and crying in pain with each blow, something made the young thug stop his attack on his woman. He turned around and faced a man about his age with a machete in his hand.

"Chill Evil, this ain't what it looks like. She tripped and fell." He said while pointing to his girl on the concrete crying all curled up in a ball.

"You know the rules," Evil said in a voice that sent chills through the young thug's spine.

"Wait no! No!" He begged and pleased with his arms out in front of him to keep Evil at a distance. Not knowing that his pleas were upon a cold heart and a deaf ear. Evil raised the machete high in the air and came down on the thug's arm and chopping his arm right off, "Ahhh!" The thug screamed as blood gushed out of his detached arm. Evil came down again on the thug's leg chopping it off at the knee, "Ahhh!" He screamed from the pain and saw it only being held together by just a piece of skin. The young thug turned on to his stomach and started crawling away using his good arm as his girl watched in horror as her man made his way to her legs where she was laying on the ground.

"Help me! Help me!" He said in a weak voice. Evil walked up to him and took off the young thug's fitted hat and bent down and said, "You know my rule." Evil stood back up and swung the machete with all his might and came down on the young thug's neck. Evil kept swinging the machete at his neck until his head rolled off. He picked up the head and placed it in a bag.

He turned and looked at the frightened woman covered in her man's blood. One of her eyes was swollen shut so she looked at Evil with her good eye. Evil put his bloody hand to his lips and motioned her to be quiet. She knew better than to talk about what happened. She knew Evil would never hit a woman, but we would kill one if he had to.

Michael Ice, Jr., or better known as Evil, walked down the street with a smile on his face, his bag in one hand, and a machete in the other. People around the neighborhood knew the rules he had. No hitting on woman in his neighborhood. It didn't matter what age or what they did. He would not see abuse on anymore woman in his lifetime again.

In the shadows, a man with a scar on his face watched the whole thing while smoking on a cigarette stuffed with crack. He smiled as he watched what the young man did to that thug. It wasn't because he was protecting that woman, but because of the mayhem and the life he took so easily. He inhaled the cigarette and laughed to himself, "Like father, like son." He said and disappeared into the shadows.

Michael Ice, Jr. jumped into a white GS Lexus and drove to a house in Flatbush, Brooklyn. His mind was playing tricks on him as he thought about what he had just done. He could still see the young thug screaming and begging for his life as he swung the machete. It wasn't his first time killing. He had done it many times before. There was something in him he could not fight. "Damn you, Black Ice. It's your blood in me that got me like this. But I swear I won't be like you. I swear." Michael yelled as a tear ran down his eye and hit the steering wheel. He grabbed the bag and walked up to the house, unlocked the door, and walked in. No one knew of this house it was one of the many properties Black Ice had owned. The only reason he had found it was because three years ago a letter came in the mail with his name on it. Inside were the title for two houses with his name on it and the set of keys. Michael never told his mother about it and when he went to see the house the things he found changed his life forever. In one house, there were money, guns, and drugs. Michael flushed all the drugs down the toilet. In the second house, were things no man or child should ever see. For many years, there have been rumors of a house that Black Ice had with nothing but body parts stashed in it like trophies. The first time Michael walked in he didn't know what to make of it. Now, it was like home. Michael walked to one of the rooms and pulled out the young thug's head and placed in a huge jar with water and put it on the shelf next to all the other victims that had met his blade. There were five rooms in the house and Black Ice had every room built into a giant freezer. There were body parts from all kind of people stuck in jars in every room from eyes to a child's hand, a man's dick, and a woman's nipples, "I can't believe this. I'm just like him," Michael said out loud as he looked around at the body parts he started to collect then left the room and the trophy house.

Chapter 2

Michael jumped in his car and was heading home. He parked his car in front of his mother's house in East Orange, New Jersey. She bought the house ten years ago with some of the money she took out of one of Black Ice's stash houses. She picked New Jersey because she felt safe and that was a hard feeling to come by, because in her heart she knew Black Ice was still alive. The police never found his body on the day he came to kill her and Janet and knowing that had her living in fear for years. At some point during the ten tears, Rachel would relapse every once in a while and would smoke crack. Michael would wander the streets for days until he found her and brought her back home. As Michael entered his mother's house, his mind raced back to the first time he killed someone. Rachel was missing for four weeks leaving Michael with her cousin. Michael cried as he stared at the door waiting for her to come back home. Janet walked up behind him and touched his shoulder on his twelve year old frame, "Don't worry Michael, she'll be back."

"No, we have to find her, she's need me," Michael said in a whisper never letting his eyes leave the door.

"But Michael, we looked everywhere and still can't find her. Go to bed and we'll try to look for her again tomorrow. Ok?"

Michael just turned his head and looked Janet in the eyes. A chill went through her body as flashbacks of Black Ice kicking and beating her almost to death and then killing the love of her life, Jay. She loved Michael, but couldn't bear to look at him in his eyes no more. He had the cold stare of his father in them. She slowly backed away and went to her room and lay on her bed crying and thinking of that deadly day.

"I can't sleep and I won't until I find you mommy. I swear," Michael rushed into his room and reached up under his bed where he kept a small machete. Then crept in his mother's room and went in her closet and found a box. In the box was a 3.80 and a 9 mm Michael always knew where his mother hid her guns. He didn't know how, but he just did. He put the 3.80 and the small machete into the book bag and left the house.

Michael and Janet had been searching four weeks for his mother all over New Jersey. Michael knew there was only one place she could be. He left the house without Janet hearing or seeing him. He walked down the block with only one goal on his mind finding his mother. He saw a cab and waved his hand for him to stop. The white cab pulled over and Michael hopped in. The tall light skin driver looked back at him. "Aren't you too young to be out this late boy?" he spoke before his eyes met Michaels. But when they did, it sent a chill through his body as if he could see and feel the evil in them.

"I'm not a boy. I am a young man and just take me to the path train in New York. That's the only business you need to worry about. The driver turned his head and took off. Once at the path train, Michael paid the driver and hopped out of the car.

He jumped on the path train heading to New York, "I'll find you, mommy. I'll find you I swear," Michael said the words over and over in his head. He got on the four train and switched over to the three train. He got off at Saratoga Avenue in Brownsville Brooklyn. It was 2am and the streets were still full with young and old drug dealers and sexy women trying to get fast money from them and crack heads everywhere buying crack and finding ways to make money to buy crack. Michael looked around. It had been years since he'd been on the streets of Brooklyn, but for some reason he felt at home. No one said nothing to him or ask him why he was out so late. He noticed in Brooklyn no one cared that there were kids younger than him out running the streets. Babies were in nothing but diapers running up and down the sidewalk, while their mothers sat on the front steps smoking weed. Michael walked five blocks down and turned right until he seen any alleyway he remembered his mother telling him about how his father killed her uncle for hurting her. Michael hid in the shadows of the night. His dark skin complexion helped him well as he watched a young thug in his twenties that came out of the alleyway. He was pulling up his jeans and to follow behind him was a young girl that looked to be no older than thirteen, "You going to give me what you promised right?" The young girl had asked while pulling up her jeans and wiping the cum off the side of her mouth.

"Shut up, I said I got you bitch," the young thug yelled while digging in his pocket and pulled out three jars crack and one bag of weed and passed it to her. "I think this is too much to give your ass, but your head is good. That's the only reason, but don't think you will get this all the fucking time," the young thug yelled.

"But you promised me one more dime of crack. This won't last long for me and my mother."

Smack! The young thug smacked the girl so hard she fell to the ground. "Now, get up and get the fuck off my block."

The young girl held her face while tears ran down her cheeks as she got up and ran off the block. The young thug stood there laughing as another crack head came into the alleyway and he gave him four dimes of crack for forty dollars.

Michael stood in the shadows with his heart racing, not out of fear, but anger as his mind flashed back. All he could see was his father's face beating his mother kicking her while she lay on the floor helpless. Michael snapped back into reality when he heard a woman's voice, "Let me get six dimes. You got me right. You know I don't have any money," she stated.

"You always go with me, Rachel, even if you had paper. It's no good here when I used to work under Caesar and Ace for Black Ice they made sure my money was right and I was good. So here I'm giving you ten dimes just come back when you're done."

"Oh shit really? Thank you," Rachel said while taking the crack and then walked away.

Michael couldn't believe his eyes. When he first heard the voice, he already knew that was her and then seeing her brought tears to his eyes. It's been a month since he seen her. "Mommy, I have to get her alone and talk to her," he said to himself as he slowly followed her to an old, all broken down house not too far from Momma's place. He watched her walk in, "This is where you are? I'll come back and get you, but first there's something I have to do," he said out loud to himself as he turned around and walked back into the shadows of the night.

"Take this crack bitch and tell your daughter I want to bust a nut tonight and to bring her ass over here if she want you to get high. Ain't shit free over here," the young thug yelled as he watched the older woman walk away.

"You give my mother crack and making her sick punk." The young thug heard the voice yell and he turned around and looked into the alleyway to see a young boy stepping out of it with a machete in his hands. He looked at the young boy up and down and laughed. "Ha ha ha ha ha ha, listen little nigga, first of all, my name is Razor. And I'll sell crack to your mother, your father, and grandmother if they come through for it. And make your mother suck my dick if I feel like it and you can't do shit about it with your big old knife. Don't you know a knife can't win a gun fight?" Razor said with a smile on his face as he pulled out a 9 mm Luger and aimed it at Michael's head.

"Don't talk about my mother like that," Michael said as he walked closer. As he stepped more out of the darkness, Razor could see his face now and see the tears. He was about to laugh, but as he seen Michael's eyes a chill went through his body as if he seen those eyes before, evil of the devil. "Go on and shoot, I have nothing to live for. If you're out here getting my mother high, she's all I have," Michael said as he stepped closer.

"Stay right there or I'll kill your ass right where you stand. Who your mother and father?" Razor asked. He hesitated on squeezing the trigger to his gun. He believed in shooting first and asks questions later. The fact was this young boy was on his block acting up was even more reason to kill him and knowing he could get away with it, but there was something about the young boy in front of him, "Oh shit! You're Black Ice's son," Razor yelled as he squeezed the trigger to 9mm luger.

Michael noticed that razor was left handed and he was now close enough to him to get one good swing with the machete. When he seen Razor squeeze the trigger, he moved to the side making the bullet just miss him as he swung with all his might. The machete came down on Razor's wrist ripping through the meat and bone, "Aahhaahah!" Razor screamed in pain as he looked down at his hand with the gun in it, hanging only by a piece of skin. Michael swung again chopping his hand completely off. "Ahhhahhh, my hand! You cut off my fucking hand!" Razor screamed in pain while crying while blood gushed out of his wrists.

Michael stood there with an evil smile on his face and watched. "That's for selling drugs to my mother punk." Razor bent over in excruciating pain. He held his wrist, but it did nothing to stop the blood from pumping fast out of him. Out of no where Razor rushed Michael and ran into him with all his body weight sending Michael to the ground and knocked the machete out of his hand. Michael looked up in shock as he seen Razor pick up a gun with his right hand and pressed what was left of his left hand to his stomach, "You fucking punk. I'm going to kill your ass. You chopped off my damn hand."

Before Razor could squeeze the trigger of his 9 mm, Boom! A shot was fired. He dropped to his knees to see Michael holding a now smoking 3.80 caliber handgun. "Ahhahah, you little punk," Razor whispered as he fell face first. Michael stood up breathing hard and picked up the machete and walked over to Razor and turned him around. Razor lay on his back with blood dripping out of his mouth and oozing out of his stomach where Michael had shot him. "You'll never be able to sell crack to my mother again asshole," he yelled as he swung the machete and chopped off Razor's right hand. "Ahhhhhh!" Razor screamed. Michael picked up Razor's cut off hand. Satisfied with his work he stuffed his hand in the book bag along with the machete and gun. "Now die slow like a crack head."

"You selling too," were the last words Razor heard as Michael walked away into the shadows. He walked back down the block and cut over and down three more blocks to the crack house where he found his mother sitting on the steps crying.

"I knew you were here, baby. I felt you. So, I waited. I knew you come for me you always do. I'm sorry, baby, it was calling to me. I couldn't help myself."

Michael took his hand and wiped his mother's tears, "Don't cry mommy. Its okay, but you have to stay strong for us. You have been doing good for so long. You don't need that stuff, mommy. Let's go home and stay strong together, mommy."

"Okay baby, you say the deepest things for your age." Michael grabbed his mother's hand and they made their way back to the train station and went home to New Jersey.

As Razor lay on the ground bleeding to death, he seen a man walk into the alleyway and stood right over him. "I did what you told me to man. I gave her free crack every time she came. Please, please help me," he said as he choked on his own blood.

The man looked at Razor and smiled his devilish grin. "Yes! Yes, you did everything I needed you to do, Razor. And you dying was part of it," the man said and laughed as he bent down and pulled out a knife that curved at the tip and cut Razor's neck from ear to ear. Then picked up his chopped off left hand and cut off the pinky finger and dropped the hand. "You won't be needing these anymore. Hahahaha," he laughed as he crept into the night.

Chapter 3

Michael snapped back to reality as he walked into his mother's house. He walked down the hall and found his mother sitting on the couch with Janet in the living room talking about God. Ever since Michael had found her that day in Brooklyn, she turned her whole life to God going to church on Mondays, Wednesdays, and Sundays.

"Janet, God is good I'm telling you. He took away my nightmares. You just keep praying and he'll take yours away too."

"I know your right, Rachel, but I can't stop dreaming of that day. I keep seeing Black Ice's face every night," Janet said as tears rolled down her face, "It's been ten years and I still can see him shoot Jay in the chest."

"Hi mom. Hi Janet," Michael said as he walked deeper into the room causing both ladies to stop their conversation and looked up at him smiling. At nineteen years old, Michael junior was 6'2" tall and weighed 200 pounds of all muscles. With his sexy dark skin complexion, he was a spitting image of his father, but was his mother loving smile at heart. At thirty nine, his mother still looked like she was in her early twenties. Her light skinned complexion glowed. She took very good care of herself. Janet was only three years younger, both women were beyond gorgeous. They could have any man they wanted, but was deeply in love with God and used that as a way to escape the pain they been through in their life.

"Junior, where have you been? Don't even

answer that, I already know. You was in Brooklyn, again."

"Yes mom, for some reason I feel at home out there," Michael replied. "Junior, if you want to go to college at Long Island University in downtown Brooklyn for human services, I'll let you go. Well, I couldn't stop you if I wanted to, but I don't want you hanging out in Brooklyn. It's a bad place for us."

"No mom, Brooklyn isn't bad. We can't blame Brooklyn because of Black Ice," Michael stated.

"Boy, you're hard headed just like your father," as soon as she said those words, Michael's face tightened. One thing he hated was to be compared to his father.

"I'm nothing like him!" Michael yelled back.

"I love you, baby, but yes you are. You have too much of him in you. I can see it. Janet can see it too. You have his cold evil eyes. The devils in you, baby," just then Rachel got up off the couch with a small bottle of holy water in her hand and she poured a few drops on her finger tips and touched his head and held it. "Devil, I repeat to leave my Son. Devil, you have no power over his body and soul. He is a child of God and belongs to him."

"Okay mama, the devil isn't in me. I don't know why you always got to do this. This is the reason I don't come home. You and Janet look at me as if I'm fucking Black Ice. I'm not him and never will be like him." Michael yelled as he walked upstairs to his room, "Damn, this is why I barely stay here. I love the shit out of my moms and Janet, but ever since they found God it's like I'm in the wrong. The son should not get punished for his father sins," Michael said out loud to himself, "I made up my mind I'm moving out this week. I can't deal with the stress." Michael lay in his bed and pulled out his sidekick and called his girlfriend.

Envy picked up on the first ring. "Hey baby, what's going on?" Envy asked.

"Everything baby, shit is crazy. I love my mom's to death, but I can't keep having her and Janet look at me as if I am like Black Ice."

"But Michael, the whole world will always look at you as if you're like your father. It's up to you to prove them wrong, baby."

"Yeah, you right baby, as always. But, I think I'm moving out this week. My mom's still don't know about the house my father left me," Michael said not telling her about the other house Black Ice had left him in Flatbush.

Michael had been with Envy for two years now. They met in school and for both of them it was love at first sight. Envy was thick in all the right spots and her fashion sense was like no other Michael had ever seen. She was always dressed to impress no matter where she was going. She matched from head to toe and had a shoe fetish. With one look at Michael's dark skin complexion, muscular frame, and his sexy smile, they hit it off right away.

"So, Michael you're willing to move in that house knowing they never found your father's body. Are you crazy, baby?"

"Naw boo, I'm not scared or worried about it. I'm not the same boy he used to be beat and torture. I'm a man now," Michael said as he touched his waist and felt two chrome 45 handguns that were there and smiled a devilish grin.

"I believe in you, Michael, so do what you see fit."

"I will baby. I will."

Chapter 4

Across town in Brownsville Brooklyn, four couples walked down the street to the twenty four hour store at lam. “I’m crazy ass drunk,” one of the women said as her man held her waist. They never even noticed a big black van following them. Four men got out and walked behind them. One of the couples man turned around, “Oh shit, that look like Black…ahhhhh,” before the man could get the name out his mouth a bullet tore the top of his head off tossing him backwards as blood flew on his girlfriend.

The three other couples turned around and all began to scream and yell as they looked at their dead friend’s brains spattered all around the concrete. They looked up to see the four men with guns aimed at them and took off running and screaming. The first shot was at one of the men in the back of his head and the bullet came out of his forehead between his eyes and bullets violently ripped and tore through the other two men’s bodies. Body parts went flying everywhere along with blood.

“Hurry up and grab the women,” one of the gunmen ordered.

“Yes boss,” the three gunmen yelled simultaneously.

Two of the girls got grabbed really fast in a choke hold from the back. The gunmen held their mouths and pulled them into the van and threw them in. The women kicked and screamed. Trying to get away, but it went in vain.

The next two women made it around the block, "I think we got away, Tiffany," one of them said as they both bent over out of breath. Out of nowhere a fist came crashing into Tiffany's face sending here flying to the ground. "Tiffany!!" her friend screamed as she watched her friend lay out with blood in her mouth on the concrete.

She looked up to see a big black man with a long scar on his face and a long gun pointed at her nose, "If you try and run again, I'm going to blow off your nose then shoot out your eyes. Do you understand me?"

The woman shook her head up and down as he grabbed her by the neck and one of the gunmen picked Tiffany up off the ground and threw her on to his shoulder as the black van spun around the block and pulled over. He tossed Tiffany in it while the man with the scar on his face dragged her friend by the neck and pushed her into the van.

Tiffany lay on the floor barely able to move. When she opened her eyes, she was praying everything that happened was a dream. But knew it wasn't when she saw her three friends', Yasmin, Jesse, and Star crying.

"Good you're ok," Star said with tears running down her face.

"Yea, but my head is spinning. Where are we?" Tiffany asked.

"I don't know where, except still in the van. Those men kidnapped us and killed our boyfriends," Star replied causing all the women to break down crying hysterically.

"We have to stay strong," Tiffany said to her

friends to give them strength.

"No Tiff, you don't know what I saw, or who I think I seen. That man that punched and knocked you out I think it could be Black Ice." Star stated.

"What?" all the women said at the same time.

Everyone knew stories or heard rumors of Black Ice with the long scar on his face, no matter what age they were. Even knowing all four women were only in their early twenties.

The van stopped. "Oh shit, I'm scared, Tiff," Star said as all four women hugged and held each other while crying.

"We must pray and stay strong. Dear God, keep us safe and protect us from this danger, in Jesus name we pray."

"Amen," they all said.

"God won't protect your ass you belong to me." The women heard a voice say then a devilish laugh as the back door of the van flew open.

They looked into the man's eyes that were standing there. They felt as if they were looking into the devil's eyes himself. The four women were dragged out the van and led into a warehouse. As soon as they entered, the strong smell of crack hit their noses. Tiffany, Star, Yasmin, and Jesse looked around as they were led deeper in and could see men dressed in all black with machine guns in their hands and what looked like a drug factory. Women were naked cooking crack cocaine and bagging it up into a Ziploc bag while the men stood on guard watching their every move.

"Tiffany, what they going to do with us?" Star asked as she held Tiffany's hand and all four of the women was pushed into a large room.

"I don't know," Tiffany replied. Tiffany and the other women looked around and noticed there were other women in the room that were naked and crying, their ankles were chained to the wall. There were fifteen women in all, laying down in fetal positions. Scared to speak or move as a huge, black man entered the room.

"What you want with us? Please, let us go!" Star cried out.

Smack! The man with the scar on his face smacked her so hard she spun around and hit the floor. "I give the fucking orders here. I'll tell you once what I want you to do and the first time you don't listen, you're dead. Do you fucking understand me?"

Tiffany and her friends cried some more and shook their heads up and down. A gunman entered the room with a metal tray with four glass pipes with lighters and crack cocaine chopped up on it. The man with the scar on his face raised his gun and aimed at all four women, "Grab the pipes ladies, and stuff them with crack and smoke."

Each of them looked at the man as if he was crazy, but nervously grabbed the crack pipes, lighters, and small pieces of crack and filled it up. "Now, light it and inhale," the man ordered.

"I can't do this shit. We're fucking drug counselors. How the hell we going to smoke crack? Kill me, do what you want, but I refuse to do this." Jesse screamed with tears.

In with one swift move, the man with a scar on his face pulled out a six inch knife that curved at the tip and slit her throat. The cut on her neck opened up and her head leaned back half way off as blood gushed out. She tried to grab her wound on her neck, but it was no use blood poured everywhere.

"Ahhhhh!!" her three friends screamed in horror and rushed to help their friend. Blood gushed everywhere as Jesse's body hit the floor. "Hold her neck! Hold her neck!" Tiffany screamed as she and Star held their friend's neck, but blood squirt all over them.

"Help us! Please, someone please help us!" Star screamed.

Then with all his might the man with the scar on his face kicked her in the jaw sending her flying backwards. The other fifteen women in the room chained to the wall cried and crawled up into a ball as they watched terrified at the new women and felt their pain. "Get away from her and let her die or you be the next one," the man yelled as he looked at Tiffany, Star, and Yasmin.

They slowly moved away from their friends body and stood up and watched her body shake and squirm around then buckle on the floor. The man with the scar on his face walked over to her body and began to saw away with his knife at her neck. "No! No!!" the women screamed and cried as they watched him rip her head off. Her body was still moving after. He stood there looking at the women with their friend's head in his hand that he held up by her hair. They could still see their friend's eyes open and lips move causing them to scream louder. "Listen, you bitches. I run this shit and what I say go. So grab those pipes and begin to smoke or you will be next."

Tiffany, Star, and Yasmin did what he said with tears running down their faces and snot dripping from their noses. They held the lighter to the tip of the glass pipe and lit and inhaled the crack smoke. Tiffany's head rushed as the crack filled her lungs and she felt dizzy. Her eyes opened up wide and her lips and body began to feel numb. The four women were forced to stand and smoke crack for three hours straight.

"You come with me," the man with the scar on his face ordered as he grabbed Tiffany's arm and pulled her out the big room dropping her friend's head on the floor.

"Tiffany, no! Don't leave us," Star screamed while standing there.

"Okay, the boss left its time for us to have our fun," one of the gunmen said as he entered the room followed by ten more men. Star and Yasmin just looked at them and fear ran through their bodies. They were higher than they ever have been in their life. A hand went around Stars neck. She tried to kick and scream, but it went in vain as the man ripped off her clothes, one man held her right leg, and another held her left leg. A man held her hands as they spread her legs. She tried to wiggle herself free knowing if she did she will hit the floor. Star's head spun some more from the crack she had been smoking and then she felt a huge dick penetrating her pussy, "AHHHHH!" she screamed and wiggled some more, but it was no use.

Each man had a good lock on the body part they were holding. The man pounded away in and out of Star, "Yes, oh yea, oh yea. You got some good pussy bitch," he groaned as he pounded hard and his men began to swing Star's body into his. They switched taken turns holding her by the arms and feet and spreading her legs, fucking her in the air. She felt as if she wanted to pass out from the pain. As she turned her head, she could see her friend Yasmin screaming and crying for help as five men took turns raping her. As they rammed them even harder, they both passed out from the pain. The man dragged them next to the wall and pulled out a long chain and locked their ankles to it.

Tiffany lay naked on a bed in a larger room crying. The man with the scar on his face had fucked her in a way she never thought could be done. She cried because part of her had enjoyed it and she shed tears for her friends who had been killed earlier in that night along with her friend, Jesse.

The man with the scar on his face sat on the edge of the bed smoking a cigarette filled crack. The crack filled his lungs and his mind raced. Tiffany looked at him with fear and hate, "You! You're Black Ice, aren't you?" she asked barely able to get the words out through her tears.

The man turned his head slowly and looked at Tiffany's naked body then her eyes. Then touched the scar on his face as his mind flashed back to the day he got it. His wife was screaming, Noooo! Noo! As he punched her in the face and she hid up under the bed. He had lifted the mattress to see her crawling on the floor. He laughed and went to reach for her when a sharp pain he felt on his hand when he tried to grab her. His wife jumped up swinging wildly and with each swing he saw more blood, but realized it wasn't her blood but his. He moved the arm he was using to block her blows as soon as he did he noticed something shiny and sharp in her hand, but it was too late the razor came down on his face, ripping it open to the white meat. His face turned pink and red as blood poured out. He grabbed his wound and his wife took off running with their son in her arms for the apartment door and down the stairs. He grabbed her just in time before she got out of the building and dragged her by her hair back into the apartment where he beat her and his son the rest of the night.

He looked at Tiffany in the eyes once more as he snapped back to reality. "Yes, I am Black Ice," he replied sending chills through her spine as he inhaled more crack smoke from his cigarette.

Chapter 5

A week later, Michael, Jr. unpacked all his things in the brownstone house in Bedford-Stuyvesant Brooklyn on Gates Avenue. “Are you sure you made the right decision by moving here and leaving your mother and her cousin?” Envy asked as she entered the room with a box in her arms.

Michael looked up at her with lust in his eyes. She had on a purple Christian Dior dress with studs in it and the high heels shoes to match. Michael smiled, loving how everything she wore always matched down to her underwear. “Yes baby. I feel I did the right thing. My mother and her cousin are safe. I’ve always had a way to feel if something is wrong with my mother. I don’t know how, but it always been that way since I was a baby. It’s been ten years and Black Ice hasn’t shown his face. He’s probably cracked out somewhere,” Michael replied. Not really believing the words he said himself about his father. He knew in his heart that Black Ice was somewhere watching him, but where he didn’t know, but would do everything in his power to find out. “We’re good, Envy, don’t stress nothing baby.” Michael said as he walked towards her, wrapped his arms around her, touched her face softly, and moved her long hair to the side. “Shit, I’m happy I got you baby. Everyone in Brooklyn thinks I’m a monster. They even named me Evil because of my father’s past.”

“Michael, they named you Evil because of the things you do when you get mad and black out or see a woman getting abused or a child getting hurt." Envy never seen him black out with her own eyes, but heard the rumors about the people he cut up when he blacked out. But, she didn't see a monster when she looked at him, just a man who been hurt as a child and loved his mother and who is very protective of the people he loved. "I don't care what people think about you, Michael. I love you and can see the real you."

Michael looked her in the eyes and kissed her deeply and passionately slowly removing the straps on her dress and letting it drop to the floor. He began to kiss her neck as she let out a soft moan. His lips traveled to her breast and took her nipple in his mouth. Envy moaned as she grabbed the back of his head. Michael's tongue moved around her nipple in a circular motion. Then he switched and began to suck the left one and taking in both of her nipples in his mouth at same time.

"Shit, god that feels so good," Envy moaned as her pussy got wetter. While he removed his clothes, he let his tongue travel down to her stomach and soon he was on his knees using his tongue to push her purple thong to the side. With one lick to her clit, her eyes rolled to the back of her head. He put his mouth around her pussy and sucked softly, beginning to suck faster and faster.

"Ohhhh god, yes, suck it baby, just like that, right there," Envy moaned as Michael sucked even faster then used his tongue to lick her clit up and down, back and forth, repeatedly making her legs shake as he licked it side to side. He took her clit and pussy lips all in his mouth at the same time sucking on it driving Envy crazy as she came, soaking her thong that was half way on. Her legs shook as he placed them on his shoulder one by one then with his strong back stood up lifting her up with him.

"Oh shit, what are you doing baby? Don't drop me," she screamed as she realized she was now in the air sitting on his shoulders with her love box all in his face while he sucked and licked her sweet pussy like there was no tomorrow. She grabbed his shoulder with one hand and held the ceiling with the other. "Oh damn! Shit, I'm cumming. I'm cumming, daddy," she screamed as she leaned her head back and allowed her sweet juices to flood his mouth and run down his chin.

Michael slowly took her off his shoulders. Envy slid down and her legs felt weak as she stood there in her 4 inch Christian Dior purple heels. He looked at her thick voluptuous body and licked his lips, "Mmm, you taste like strawberries, baby." Michael said.

"Hmmm really," Envy replied as she turned around and held the wall. She turned her head to look at his hard nine inch, dark chocolate dick, and sexy muscled body up and down. He gripped her hips and slowly inserted the tip of his dick inside her, "Damn that pussy wet, baby."

"It's all wet for you, daddy," Envy moaned as he pushed his dick deeper and deeper inside her while passionately kissing down her back. "Owwww damn, baby. Shit, fuck me," she screamed.

The sweet sensation of his dick hitting her

walls teasing and pleasing her on each stroke sent chills up and down her spine. He went deeper and deeper. Envy yelled as he pounded away. He grabbed her hair and smacked her ass repeatedly. She screamed as she looked back at his body glistening in sweat.

"Who you love?" Michael yelled then bit down on his bottom lip.

"I love you, daddy," she moaned as she rotated her waist stimulating her pussy even more and making her cum for the fourth time. Michael pounded as hard as he could and pulled out nutting all over her ass. "Shit, my legs are weak and I still feel that dick all up in my stomach, damn," Envy stated.

"Well sexy I'm not done with you yet," Michael replied while leading her to the bed and spread her legs taking her clit in his mouth once more making her legs shake.

Outside across the street, was a man standing in the dark and had watched Michael and Envy spend the day moving in to the brownstone house. He stood in the dark the whole night to see if they would ever leave the house. But, they didn't. Their night was spent making love.

Chapter 6

Michael jumped in his car and drove to Brownville, Brooklyn. For the last two years, he took most of the money he found in the house Black Ice had left him and bought Abonda School on Blake Avenue and Rockaway right in the projects. He had rebuilt it into a community center for abused women and women on drugs, young children, and teens to have a place to go to for food, a place to sleep, and also help them get away from the streets. He circled the neighborhood four times to see who was hustling. He had made a strong rule in the neighborhood telling all drug dealers they weren't allowed to sell drugs in a fifteen block radius of the community center. And no man in the neighborhood was allowed to put his hands on a woman in anyway, beating or hitting them. At first all the older hustlers took him as a joke and didn't listen until they started popping up dead with missing body parts along with men that were beating their women. That's when they realized he was the son of Black Ice, no matter how nice he may seemed or how much good he may do. He had his father's blood in him and was truly evil. So the name stuck and every hustler, or thug, and women beater knew him by it and feared him.

Michael pulled up in the parking lot and hopped out of his car, never noticing the two men standing by the corner store in all black watching his every move as he entered the center. "You make your move first, as soon as he leaves, that's when you get him. Do you understand me?" the older man said to the younger one.

"Yea, this will be the last night Evil will walk on this earth," the young one replied.

"Hey, what's up boss?" Dashawn said as Michael walked in.

"Nothing much, how is it looking today?" Michael replied.

Dashawn was one of the several counselors he had working for him. "I never seen it this packed, Michael. I have never seen so many women looking for help," Dashawn replied.

Michael walked deep in and began to do his rounds, walking around and checking on everything. The community center was a school that had three floors. The first floor was intake, where the women and children would check in and would meet with a counselor. There was a gym in further back along with a movie room and a game room. The second floor was the cafeteria and showers, where any woman and child could come off the street to eat and use the showers to stay clean. If they were in problems to get clean off drugs or get away from abusive men, they came to the community center. The third floor was a huge housing area with a hundred and ten beds.

Michael only took in women and children because all the things he seen and been through with his mother. As he entered the cafeteria, he couldn't believe his eyes at all the little boys and girls sitting down eating and how skinny they were. His mind flashed back on how he wouldn't eat for days because his mother forgot to feed him or buy food. Michael walked back to his office and called for one of his counselors, "Kevin, what's going on? I've never seen so many people."

"It's worse. Michael, have you noticed that all the women smoking crack is younger now, from the age fourteen to thirty and their pregnant. That's crazy our generation didn't smoke crack, maybe weed here and there. But, mostly people in the 80's smoke crack. So why are more crack heads popping up and why mostly women when drugs been slowly down for the last few years.

Michael took a second to think about what Kevin had said and knew he was right. There have been more and more young women getting addicted to crack in the neighborhood and also how a lot of the women had gone missing and would pop back up after a few months, but others would never be seen again like his four friends that also worked as counselors at his center. Tiffany, Star, Yasmin, and Jesse haven't been seen for well over three weeks now and the police had no clue where to look or what happened to them or if they really cared.

While Kevin and Michael were talking, a little boy knocked on the door, "Well, you know who that is boss? We'll finish this conversation later," Kevin said as he got up and left the office.

And the little boy entered, "Hey, what's up Michael?" the boy said as he sat in a chair in front of Michael's desk.

"Nothing much, Mike. How are you doing today?" Michael replied while smiling.

Mike put his head down unable to speak. For a whole year, he had been coming to the center faithfully and for some reason he felt a connection right away with Michael. He felt he could tell him all his problems and he would be the only one to really understand him. At ten years old, Mike had been through more pain than a little. His mother was a crack head who died giving birth to him. He was told and ever since he was raised in different foster homes. In each one, he was beaten and abused and left without food. The last home he had to leave though was the best. When Mike first got there two years ago, he thought Ms. Maxwell was the sweetest old woman in the world. He soon found out the truth. The money the state was giving her to take care of him, to buy clothes and food, she was using it to buy crack. And left Mike wearing the same clothes for days and there was no food. If it wasn't for the community center, he wouldn't eat at all or been able to wash the little bit of clothes he did have.

"I was taking a shower and Miss Maxwell came in to the bathroom high, Michael, with an extension cord and beat me. I screamed and cried, but she kept on beating me," Mike stated.

"What, I'm going over there now," Michael yelled with anger because looking at Mike he seen so much of himself in him. He had the same dark skin complexion and the same deep cold eyes filled with pain and anger.

"It's too late, she's dead, Michael."

"What you mean she's dead?"

"Promise you won't tell on me."

"What Mike? What happened? You got my word. I won't say nothing to nobody, now tell me."

"I killed her last night," Mike replied.

"What?" Michael yelled.

Mike looked up and then moved around in the chair. "I got tired of her beating me. She beat me bad, Michael. I was sore and really hurt. I was crying for hours. No one loves me. My mother didn't love me enough to stop smoking crack while pregnant with me and every foster home I go to they beat me and don't feed me and make me sleep on the floor or the stairs while they treat their kids so nice and kind. I hate my life," Mike said while crying using his little hands to wipe away his tears.

"Don't say that. And don't cry. I know how you feel I'm here for you," Michael replied thinking of his life and how he used to feel the same way. "So, how did you kill her? The police will be looking for you."

"No, I killed her in a way they can't prove I did it. I broke glass up in tiny small pieces and stuffed it in her glass crack pipe. When she went to get high, she choked on the glass and it cut up her throat and lungs and I watched her fall to the ground and spit up blood and reach out for me. I looked at her and smiled and when I was sure she was dead, I called the cops and they came. The police said she overdosed and choked on her own glass pipe. And ACS had to take me to another home. So, I took off running and been here ever since last night."

Michael's mind raced as it flashbacked and he remembered the same thing he did to his father and it would have worked if it wasn't for his mother saving his life. "You can't keep hiding, Mike, you have to go to ACS so they can find you another home," Michael replied.

"No, I don't want to. I'm tired of going from home to home and getting beat in every home I've been in for no reason because my mother was a crack head. I'll stay here. I got food here and get to play with the other kids," Mike replied.

"This isn't the place to raise a child, Mike. I opened this place for kids and women to get away from the streets and know there's someone to help them in the hood."

"I don't want to go, Michael. I'll run."

"Okay Mike, but I don't want you to stay here. Come home with me tonight and we'll talk about what we are going to."

"Uhmmm, what about your mother do you think she is mad that I'm staying there?" Mike asked.

"Naw, I live with Miss Envy, now. You remember her right?"

"Yeah I do. I like her. She dress really nice and she's funny."

"Yea, I know I just got to discuss you staying there with us. If I don't tell her and we pop up, that will be both our butts that will get in trouble." Mike and Michael both busted out laughing knowing it were true.

Later on that day, Michael said bye to most of his workers and people in the center and headed out the door with Mike by his side. With one look at the two of them, you'd swear Mike was his son. As they walked to his 97 white Lexus GS, he dialed Envy's number. "Hey daddy, how was your day?" Envy asked as soon as she answered the phone.

"It was good baby girl, but I have to talk

with you when I get home. Also wanted to let you know, I'm bringing little Mike home with me tonight," Michael said.

"Okay, but why? What's going on?" Envy replied.

"That's what I have to talk to you about, boo."

"Alright baby, I'm happy you let me know, because I was waiting for you with my red corset on and no panties."

Michael busted out laughing, "You know what I like." Michael was so deep into his conversation he didn't see the four men dressed in black following him to his car. Mike had seen them crossing the street and put his hand in his pocket where he kept his 4inch switch blade pocketknife. Growing up in different foster homes, he taught himself to stay on point and always carry a knife, or kept something on him to protect himself.

The first gunmen was now two feet from the back of Michael as he pulled out a chrome Heckler 9mm and aimed it at the back of his head. Mike looked back and pulled out his knife and flipped it open. The gunmen began to squeeze the trigger to his gun slowly, but in one swift move, Michael dropped his cell phone and pulled out twin Koch 45 handguns and squeezed the trigger to both guns simultaneously. At the same time Mike had swung hard, his knife went into the gunmen's thigh. Before the gunmen could scream, bullets of the 45 slammed into his chest and face sending him flying backwards. Mike looked up at Michael with shock in his eyes as he held his now bloody knife. In no way did he think Michael was paying any attention to the men, but he had seen them.

Once they had left the center and were anticipating their next move, "Run!" Michael yelled as he watched the first gunmen go down and could see three others now with their guns out and aiming at him and Mike. Michael took aim and squeezed the trigger of his guns, as bullets went past his head. Fire of orange and red blast came out the muzzle of his guns, bullets slammed into one of the gunmen's stomach. He bent over in pain to only have a bullet explode his head like a melon. Michael and Mike ducked for cover as the other two gunmen exchanged fire bullets that ripped and tore into park cars that Mike and Michael were using for cover. One of the gunmen slowly crept on the side of them, making sure to stay low using trees in the parking lot of the projects. Michael dodged and ducked and returned fire at the gunmen that was using the bus stop as cover. Michael stood up with anger racing through his body and aimed and squeezed the trigger of the twin 45 handguns. A hail of bullets crashed through the glass windows of the bus stop and metal pole and hit the gunmen ripping chunks of his flesh out of his face. His body jerked as bullets went through it and came out his back. He fell face first with half of his face gone. Before Michael could look around for the last gunmen, he felt the barrel of a gun at the back of his head, "Drop your fucking guns, Michael."

"Damn!!" Michael cursed out loud, knowing it was over he was caught off guard.

"You didn't hear me, Michael, drop the

fucking guns or will you listen better if I called you Evil."

'Damn, I'm wondering who the fuck he is.' Michael thought to himself as he dropped his guns and slowly turned around and couldn't believe his eyes.

"Yea motherfucker, you forgot all about me, but I never forgot about you. Get on the fucking ground."

"Pooky, that you?" Michael asked as his mind flashed back to when he was a child and had to live at Momma's house with all the other kids or 'children of a crack momma,' Momma used to call them. All the children were related in some way and Pooky was his cousin that he was forced to share a bed with. But, Pooky would pee the bed every night leaving Michael soaked in his urine. Michael got fed up with it and told Pooky he had to sleep on the floor. When he refused, Michael beat him up and left him on the floor for that day. Pooky was never allowed to get in the bed with him and there was nothing he could do to change that. "Pooky, what the fuck you doing? You're my cousin. We're family you ass. You're still holding on to some shit that happened when we was kids?"

"Shut up, Evil, and lay on the ground."

Michael was on his knees and laid flat on his stomach while Pooky kept the gun pointed at him. Pooky unzipped his jeans and pulled out his dick and begun to pee all over Michael. "Just like old times, huh Evil," Pooky said while shaking his dick making sure to empty his bladder, "Yea, you evil fucker. I got you now and when I kill you the hood will fear me and I'll take the respect that should be mines."

"You mother fucker!" Michael yelled as anger rose in his body and spit urine out of his mouth.

Pooky smiled not paying attention to little Mike, who was hiding under a parked car the whole time. He crawled from under the car and climbed on top of the hood. He looked at Pooky's back and jumped on it. "Oh shit!" Pooky yelled trying to shake Mike off his back. Mike pulled his arm all the way back, the one with the knife in it, and swung with all his might aiming for Pooky's neck, but missed. The knife penetrated his ear going straight through the hole, ripping through the flesh as it hit his ear drum busting it. "Ahhhh!" Pooky screamed louder than any man Mike had ever heard.

Michael turned around and pulled out a 12 inch knife he strapped to the side of his thigh under his jeans. He swung at Pooky's dick that was still out. The sharp blade went up and cut the head of Pooky's dick off causing him to drop his gun and trying to bend over in pain and shake Mike off at the same time.

Mike flew off of Pooky's back and hit the concrete and looked at his knife covered in blood. Michael jumped up and grabbed his guns and his phone. Stared a devilish look at Pooky lying on the ground, one hand holding his dick and the other hand holding his ear as he screamed and cried and pain while blood soaked the concrete. Michael seen an empty plastic bag and used it to pick up the head of Pooky's dick then put it in his pocket. He aimed his gun at Pooky's head, "Now, it's time for you to die. You pee in the bed motherfucker."

The older man in the dark had seen enough he pulled out a black uzi and aimed and squeezed the trigger. A hail of bullets went out of control and hit the car next to Michael and the buildings. Michael dove to the ground as bullets whispered pass his ear. Mike followed Michael as they crawled into his car and he started it up and pulled off as bullets hit the back of the car and window as he made it down the block and around the corner.

The old man walked over to Pooky and looked down at him rocking back and forth holding his wounds and his dick as blood pumped from them. "You fuck, Pooky. Don't know how you couldn't have finished the job, but you get another chance," the older man said as he picked Pooky up off the ground and threw him up on his shoulders and into a car and drove off slow as police cars started to fill the block.

Michael drove like a mad man. He pulled up to the house in Flatbush and pulled the car into the garage. Inside it was a matching GS Lexus, but black. Michael looked at Mike and almost forgot he was there. Mike's facial expressions showed no emotion. 'Damn, for a ten year old, you'd think he'd be crying or in shock, but he's just sitting there like nothing happen,' Michael thought.

"Mike, I need you to go sit in the black car right there and give me a second to run in the house really fast okay?"

Mike shook his head up and down. They got out the car at the same time as Mike got in and sat in the passenger seat of the black GS Lexus while Michael used the door that was connected to the garage to go inside the house. He went upstairs turned on a light once he stepped into the room he grabbed a jar filled with water and pulled out the plastic bag that was in his pocket and dumped the head of Pooky's dick into it and closed it and placed it on the shelf next to all the other trophies he collected. He shut off the light and locked the room door and went back downstairs into the garage and jumped in the car and took off. 'I hope he don't remember the address to this house. I wasn't supposed to bring anyone here, but had to drop that off,' Michael thought to himself as he stopped at a red light and looked at Mike. Then he pulled off.

"Mike, you know we can never tell anyone about what happened tonight just like the thing that happened to your foster mother. You understand?"

"Yes, I understand Michael. I won't say a word."

"Mike, why wasn't you scared or why you didn't run away? Any other kid your age would have?" Michael asked while driving and looking at Mike from the corner of his eyes wondering why this little boy was so calm.

"I don't know I just wasn't scared and where was I supposed to go if I ran? ACS will find me and just take me to another foster home where they will beat me and won't feed me." Mike replied.

Michael's mind flashed back to when he was a child and how Black Ice used to beat him and his mother for days on days. So much of this little boy reminded Michael of himself even the look in his eyes when he jumped on Pooky's back and stabbed him in the ear. He looked like he was enjoying it. It couldn't be maybe I was seeing things Michael thought to himself as pushed the thoughts out of his mind.

Michael pulled up on his block on Gates Avenue and found parking. Mike and him got out of the car and walked to his brownstone house. "So, this is where you live? I like it," Mike said smiling.

"Yea, this is where me and Envy both live," Michael said as he opened the front door.

"Baby, that you?" Envy asked as she stuck her head out from the dining room. "I cooked chicken, rice, peas, and grill shrimps," she said as she walked out wearing a black Chanel dress and a red belt with red Chanel heels. Her brown skin gave off a glow as she smiled at them then her facial expressions changed as she seen blood on Michael's clothes and on Mike's clothes as well. She ran to Mike and bent down checking him for cuts and wounds and did the same to Michael. "Baby, what happened? What happened?" she asked with tears in her eyes and concern in her voice, "And why are you wet and smell like pee?"

"Envy, baby I'll tell you everything, but let me jump in the shower fast and see if you can find something for him to put on. In the morning we'll take him shopping to get some new things," Michael said as he went upstairs into the bathroom and jumped in the shower. He let the hot water run over his body to clear his mind.

Chapter 7

As his nine inch dick penetrated her pussy, she let out a slight moan and wrapped her arms around his back feeling his muscles with each stroke of his chocolate dick turning the pain into pleasure as he sucked on her neck and nipples. "Spread your legs," he ordered. She did what he told her to and her pussy got moister with each stroke, "Oohhhh," she moaned.

"Yesss! Yes. You love this dick don't you? Don't you!" he yelled as he lifted her up and turned around and lay on his back. She began to ride his dick with all her might. Soon she was slipping and sliding, up and down his dick effortlessly from the wetness. 'Oh god, why does he feel so good inside me,' she moaned as she closed her eyes enjoying the feeling of his stiffness. The thickness of his dick filled her up. Her hips shook and she began to quiver and try to move, but stopped as she came, "Damn! Damn!" She slowly rolled her hips then her body was quivering uncontrollably as a gush of her juices ran out of her and on to his dick and thighs.

"Now, really give me that pussy," the man demanded as she lay down on to his chest and he began to pound faster and harder. "Spread your ass! Spread your ass!" he screamed. She reached her hands to the side while lying on his chest and spread her butt cheeks, "Shit fucks me! Fuck me!" she screamed as she was unable to control herself thrusting her body against his. "Shit! Oh my god!" she screamed once more as she felt him expand and cum inside her. Her finger nails dug into his chest as he pounded even harder and faster until they both came five times and were exhausted. She lay on her stomach.

He looked at her caramel skin complexion and fat ass and his dick was hard as a rock once more as he climbed on top of her and placed two of his fingers in her mouth and gave her long deep strokes from the back. "You like that? Don't you love this dick?" he groaned with each stroke, grinding around in a circle.

"Ohhohh shit! Yesss...yes baby! I do," she moaned while sucking on his fingers. He pounded one last time really hard and deep and pulled out busting a nut all over her ass. "That's my pussy and don't ever fucking forget it."

He crawled off the bed and sat at a table and filled two glass pipes with crack than passed one to her with a lighter. He held the lighter to the tip of his glass pipe and inhaled the thick white crack smoke and held it in than exhaled.

Tiffany watched his muscled up chocolate body then held the lighter to the pipe and inhaled the crack smoke as tears stream down her face. 'How the fuck am I loving his dick inside me? He killed my man and Jesse and got me smoking crack. And I don't know if Star and Yasmin are still alive. I've been trapped in this room for damn near two months I think. I miss my family,' She cried some more and looked up to see Black Ice staring at her. She quickly tried to stop crying and wipe her tears. But, it was too late.

"What the fuck have I told you about crying,

Roxy?"

"My name isn't Roxy. And no please don't hit me again. I'm sorry," Tiffany cried out and tried to use the sheets to cover her body knowing they'd give her no real protection. Black Ice picked up his jeans off the floor and pulled his belt loose.

"You want to cry I'll give your ass something to cry for bitch," he walked over to the bed and swung. The belt hit her across the face.

"Ahhhh, stop, please stop!" Tiffany screamed as she put up her hands to block the blow.

Black Ice ripped the sheet off her body and continued to swing with all his might. "Roxy, I told your ass about running away. I told you about crying and fucking other men."

"AHHHH, I'm not Roxy!" Tiffany cried out as the belt hit her head and legs.

"Oh you still want to talk?" Black Ice flipped the belt over and began to be beat her with the belt buckle. The belt buckle ripped through her flesh on her arms and legs. "I'll call you whatever I like bitch and you won't say shit. Do you her me?"

"Yes! Yes!" Tiffany cried out hysterically. Black Ice was unsympathetic to her pleas and tears and beat her until she passed out from the pain.

Chapter 8

Tiffany woke up the next morning her body swollen and in pain. Bruises were all over her face and her ribs felt fractured. Tears slowly streamed down her face. She wanted to cry out loud, but could feel the evil presence of Black Ice in the room. She wiped her tears while up under the sheets and peeked her head out to see Black Ice sitting on a couch across the room.

To be in a warehouse, the room was luxurious and more like a studio apartment from the cream couch set to the black carpet and king sized bed, she was forced to sleep in, to the four 52 inch TVs and she noted Black Ice used two of them to watch the huge warehouse with cameras. She was never allowed to look at those monitors.

Tiffany looked low at the little lump on her belly and wanted to cry all over again. In her heart she knew she was pregnant and it belonged to the monster, calling himself a man, sitting on the couch looking at her. 'I can't go on like this no more. My body ached I been forced to smoke crack, and use it to ease my pain. I been here for two months or longer I can't tell. And I still don't know what's going on or why I am here and why he keeps calling me Roxy. I don't care if he beats me or kill me. I won't live like this,' Tiffany thought to herself as she got out of the bed and walked into the bathroom. She took a shower as the water hit her skin, her bruises stung. When she was done, she got dressed and put on some leggings and a black tank top. One thing about Black Ice she noticed, he kept new clothes for her. ‘Is this all part of his plan?’ she thought to herself as she made her way over to the couch where he was sitting, smoking a cigarette mix with crack dressed in all black.

He looked at her suspiciously as she sat down next to him. Then he smiled his devilish grin as he looked at her stomach. “Smoke this!” he ordered passing her a rolled up blunt filled with purple haze weed and crack.

Tiffany took the blunt nervously and looked at it. ‘I don’t want to smoke this shit no more, but it keep calling me and my body ache so bad and if I don’t he’ll beat me again.’ She thought to herself as water filled her eyes. She lighted the blunt inhaled then exhaled the smoke out. She sat there for a few minutes before working up the nerves to ask him questions on things she needed to know.

“Uhmm, I know you’re going to be beat for asking, but I have to know these things even if you do.”

Black Ice looked at her with a cold stare than smiled. It was the first time she ever really spoke up for herself. One thing he respected was people with no fear for death or life, but also he fed off fear. He laughed out loud, “Sure ask whatever you want to know, bitch, it won’t make a difference. You're mines for life or as long as I want you.”

Tiffany inhaled the thick smoke one more time and tried not to be scared or let his words get to her. “Okay, why do you keep calling me Roxy? I know it’s not a nickname that you call me because when you’re really high I swear you really think I am her.” Black Ice facial expressions changed. She could see the anger in it as he thought of her question.

"The reason you're in this room with me and not with the rest of the bitches is because you look just like Roxy from your caramel skin complexion and your thick, sexy hourglass shape even your face. She's the reason I started smoking crack," Black ice replied.

"How was she the reason you started smoking crack and what happened to her?" Tiffany asked listening deeply.

Black Ice lighted another cigarette mix with crack and exhaled the smoke from his nose. "I wanted Roxy, but she wanted nothing to do with a drug dealer. So, I tricked her when we chilled out one night. I put crack in her weed, but like you, she was no fool. I had to smoke with her and that was the beginning of the end. What happened to her is she ran away from me and no one can get away from me unless I allow them to. I shot her in the head when I found her and she was seven months pregnant. Ha ha ha ha ha ha," Black ice said and busted out laughing. "So, if you have any thoughts or ideas of ever running and getting away know I will find you and chop off your fucking head like I did your friend."

Tiffany didn't know if she wanted to cry or punch him in the face, but had to hold her composer. "The next thing I'd like to know is why you kidnap me and my friends and all those other women and force us to smoke crack?"

Black ice busted out laughing once more. His laugh sent chills down her spine, "How old are you, Tiffany?"

"I'm twenty three years old."

"Okay, I'm forty."

'He's forty with a body that looked like that Tiffany thought she thought for sure he was in his thirties,' Tiffany thought to herself.

"So, how many crack heads you know your age?" Tiffany took her time to think about the question.

"Well, not many. My generation don't really smoke crack just weed because we seen the affect it had on our parents and other older family members. But, there have been a few more women lately my age hooked on to drugs," Tiffany replied looking at him with a blank stare.

"That's the whole point, bitch. There isn't much people your generation that do smoke crack because the affect it will have. But back in the eighties, no one knew there was money every where for drug dealers. So I came up with a plan to kidnap women in your generation and younger and whoever else I feel like. I keep them here for as long as I like get them addicted on to crack and if they refuse, well you know what will happen. They die like your friend. And that's not even the best part, I have my men fuck them and see how many of them can get pregnant and we will have a generation of crack babies. That will bring more business for me. I have my men sell kilos and bricks of crack cocaine to all the drug dealers making me rich." Black Ice smirked as he thought of how smart he was.

Tiffany sat in deep thought as her mind

wondered, 'How many women had he done this to? It's all clear now why there were more women my age smoking crack. How long had he been doing this and he had his men rape the women? Oh shit, Star and Yasmin that means they have been raped too.'

"Nooo!" she screamed out loud and wanted to cry, but knew better. "Can I see my friends? Please are they still alive?"

"You want to see your friends? Yea, they're still alive," Black Ice replied with his evil grin. "But, first you know what to do and do it how I like or I'll punch you in your fucking face," he said as he pulled out his nine inch dick.

Tiffany wiped the two tears going down her face and grabbed his dick and began to jerk it up and down. She bent over and slowly took it all in to her mouth and began to suck it up and down.

"Ahhh shit, yes like that Roxy," Black Ice moaned as he grabbed the back of her head and pushed it all the way down and up, fucking her mouth like it was pussy. She began to suck the tip of his dick head and his eyes rolled to the back of his head from the sweet sensation of her mouth. She began to suck his balls placing them in her mouth one at a time then both at once. The whole time she wished she could bite his nuts off or dig her fingernails into his eyes, but knew she would be dead soon after. She swallowed that extra saliva in her mouth and let her tongue travel up and down the shaft of his dick and wrapped her lips around it. She twisted her head around while sucking up and down and going faster and faster. "Oh shit," Black

Ice moaned loudly as he ejaculated in her mouth. She sucked even harder as she felt the warm cum run down her throat and swallowed it all. "Damn, that was good Roxy."

Tiffany lifted up her head and wiped her mouth, "May I see my friends now, please?"

"Yea," Black Ice replied as he stuffed his dick back into his jeans, "Come follow me."

Tiffany got off the couch and followed him to a big steel door where he entered a code and the door popped open. She followed him down the hall. She could see gunmen everywhere. It was her first time being out of the room in months. She made sure to pay attention to every door and looked for an exit. 'I don't remember seeing all this when he first brought me,' she said to herself as she entered the elevator and seen him press b, for basement. 'Ok this warehouse has two floors and a basement,' she thought to herself as she took mental notes. They got off the elevator and walked down the hall passed four large doors and stopped in front of one with two gunmen standing in front of it. "Open the fucking door," Black Ice ordered.

"Yes, boss," one of the gunmen said as he entered a code and the lager steel door popped open.

Black Ice walked in with Tiffany following. The room was large and dark and smelled of urine and crack. Tiffany looked around curiously as she couldn't believe her eyes. There were more than twenty five women chained to the wall all around the room and she could see some of the gunmen having sex with them, some three or four at a time. Some women sitting and others were standing smoking endless supply of crack in front of them. And worse a lot of them were pregnant. Tiffany continued to follow Black Ice. Then her eyes met with a young girl that looked to be no more than fourteen years old and six months pregnant. She had a glass crack pipe to her lips and was taking deep pulls of the thick white smoke. "You two get off now," Black Ice yelled at two of his henchmen that were fucking a woman in the corner.

Tiffany took her eyes off the fourteen year old girl to see who Black Ice was yelling at. Her body began to tremble in horror as she watched the two men pull up their pants and get off her friend Star. Star stood up and picked up her long T-shirt off the floor and put it back on and sat back down. She picked up her glass pipe and took pieces of crack off a small metal tray that was in front of her and began to smoke never paying any mind to Black Ice and Tiffany standing there. "Go ahead and talk to your friends," Black Ice said as he smiled his devilish grin and looking at his work.

Tiffany ran over to her friend, "Star! Star, what are you doing? Are you okay?" Star looked up at Tiffany kneeling down at her and put down the crack pipe.

"Tiffany, is that you? I must be fucking high. Yo, Yasmin I think I see Tiffany again and am I smoking too much?"

Tiffany looked to her left two feet away and couldn't believe it. Yasmin was sitting on the floor smoking. "Oh shit! I think I see her too, girl," Yasmin replied.

Tiffany took Star's hand, "It's me, Star. I

am here."

"Oh my, Lord! It's really you, Tiffany," Star and Tiffany hugged. Yasmin came over and the three women hugged and cried. Tiffany broke their embrace and looked at them. The crack they have been smoking have ate away at all their body fat. They were skinny in the face and had blemishes. Yasmin and Star had on nothing but a long white T-shirt to cover their bodies. 'I can't believe this. My best friends are full blown crack heads,' Tiffany thought to herself.

"Tiffany, where have you been? We thought you was dead," Star stated. Tiffany lowered her head. So many times she wished she was dead from being trapped in that room and being raped by Black Ice and forced to smoke crack. Her mother used to always say 'no matter how bad your situation is there's always someone in the world doing worse'. She now knew that was true. Here I am stressing and crying because I'm being beat and raped by Black Ice, but stay in a room as big as an apartment full of luxury and sleeping on a bed while my friends are being raped by five different men every day and sleeping on the floor.

"No, I'm not dead even though I wish I was many times. I been with the man with the scar on his face and you were right he is Black Ice."

"I knew it!" Star shouted.

"Star, you want to hit this?" Yasmin said passing Star a glass pipe filled with crack. Star held the lighter to it and inhaled deeply the thick smoke. She passed the glass pipe with more crack. "Here Tiffany hit this," Star said passing the pipe.

"I want to, but I can't," Tiffany said fighting the urge to get high. And what was even sadder was to see that her friends were now smoking on their own free will and now addicted.

"Tiffany, what's going on? Why are we being kept here? I don't even know how long we've been here. I just keep smoking to fight the pain of what these men do to us every day and from missing my family. I see some women and girls leave here and never come back. I think they kill them and bring new girls and women in. Tiffany looked back just to make sure Black Ice was nowhere near them. He was walking off and talking to some of his henchmen and was looking at some of the other women.

"Star and Yasmin, I need you two to stay strong. I'm going to find us a way out of here."

"How?" Star asked not believing it.

"I don't know. But I will. Black Ice uses this place to bring women and get them addicted to crack and pregnant then sets them free and it brings him more business because there's a new generation of crack heads," Tiffany replied.

"So, that's what they've been doing?" Yasmin said really getting into the conversation for the first time.

"I think I'm pregnant," Tiffany said looking at her stomach.

"Me too," Yasmin added.

"I am too. So what are we going to do?" Star asked.

"Don't worry I have a plan. We just have to be ready okay. I'm going to try to get us out of here real soon. Every other Wednesday, Black Ice has a meeting with henchmen and workers and once every month they go and kidnap new women. One of those days when their busy, that's when we will escape. Try your hardest to stay clean and not smoke and get too high. We're going to need clear heads when it happens."

"Alright Tiffany I'm with you," Star replied. Yasmin looked at Star then Tiffany and put her glass pipe to her lips and inhaled more thick white crack smoke. "Yea, I'm done even though I think the two of you are fucking crazy," she said while talking with smoke still in her lungs.

"Being fucking crazy is the only way we're going to get the fuck out of here. They may let the other women and girls go, but I have a feeling Black Ice isn't going to ever let us go free, unless it's in a body bag," Tiffany stated while looking in both her friends eyes.

"Tiffany, your time is up," a voice boomed. Tiffany looked behind her to see Black Ice coming for her. He grabbed her by the arm. "It's fucking time to go."

"Bye I love you both," she yelled while being dragged out the lager room.

"We love you too, Tiffany," Star and Yasmin shouted back.

Chapter 9

Michael, Envy, and little Mike spent the morning shopping for clothes for him and then stopped at IHOP. Mike sat down at the table and looked at Michael and Envy. He never felt so good in his life. "Thank you Michael and Ms. Envy for the clothes. No one has ever been so kind to me."

"It's okay, baby. We did it because we want you to be happy," Envy replied.

"Yea, so what would you like to eat?" Michael asked.

"Uhmm, I want strawberries on my pancakes with eggs and bacon and can I have a strawberry milkshake too, please?"

"Sure baby, you can have anything you want," Envy stated. 'Damn, he reminds me so much of Michael. He have the same cold eyes filled with pain and at the same time look like their full of love,' Envy thought to herself.

"I think I'll have the same thing too," Michael stated.

"Oh yeah, I called ACS and spoke to a social worker and she said all they have to do is come look at our house and from there they will give us the answer if you can stay with us from now on. Would you like that Mike?" Envy asked.

"What? Yes, I'll love that," Mike replied while stuffing his mouth with pancakes causing Envy and Michael to burst out laughing then smiled at each other.

"Mike, I'm just happy were done shopping. Fashion is like a drug to Envy she'll have us shopping all day if she could."

"Shut up, Michael," Envy said and kissed him.

Mike just smiled. He never had been around people so kind and loving. "Okay, after we finished eating we'll go visit my mom."

"Okay, that be nice baby it's been a week since you seen her."

"Yea, that's the longest I've been away from her. I don't like being away from her even though she drives me crazy just like you, baby."

"Shut up, Michael," Envy said as all three of them got up and left IHOP.

Michael drove in silence with everything on his mind from his cousin and those men trying to kill him last night to him now taken Mike in his and Envy's life and missing his mother and wondering if she was safe, but in his heart he knew she was. He took a quick look at Envy and then looked at the backseat at Mike and could see both of them were asleep. He slowly pulled up to his mothers East Orange, New Jersey house. "We're here," he said as both Mike and Envy woke up. Mike looked all around at the house and the neighborhood. Envy stepped out of the car and walked to the trunk and opened it and took out a bag. She followed Michael and Mike to the house door. Michael used his keys to open the door and walked in followed by Mike and Envy. Food could be smelled from the kitchen. "Junior, my little man is that you?" Rachel called out.

"Yes, mom it's me," Michael replied. Michael walked into the kitchen to see his mother cooking and Janet helping set up the table. “Hey mommy, I miss you,” Michael said as he kissed her on the cheeks. “Hi Janet,” he said and kissed her as well.

“Hi Miss Ice,” Envy said.

“Oh baby, I didn’t see you. I can feel when my boy is around and you know to call me mom,” Rachel replied as she kissed Envy on her cheeks.

“We got something for you mom,” Envy said and passed her the bag.

Rachel opened it to see a blue church dress with a big blue church hat to match. “Awww, thank you babies,” she said and kissed them both. “Oh who is this little guy?” Rachel asked as she noticed Mike for the first time.

“This is Mike mom. He’s from Brownsville Brooklyn. Me and Envy decided to take care of him for awhile.”

“Hi Miss Rachel,” Mike said speaking for the first time.

“Hey baby,” Rachel said bending down to get a better look at him. Her eyes opened up wide when she did. He looked just like Michael even down to his eyes she thought to herself. “Michael, Envy, come with me,” she said as she stood up and walked towards the basement door with Michael and Envy following her.

The basement was dark. Rachel hit the light switch and turned around to face Michael and Envy. “Baby, the devil is coming for you.”

“Mom, are you going to start talking about that devil stuff? Please don’t start talking that bullshit. I didn’t come for this.”

"Baby, this is no bullshit. The signs are clear. God has shown me in my dreams and that boy upstairs is another sign you need to get away from him, baby."

"Mom, you're bugging."

"Michael, I'm not fucking bugging as you say. You have a gun baby?' Rachel asked while touching his waist and feeling his 45 handgun there. Envy eyes opened up wide with shock. She never had seen a mother that wanted her son to carry a gun. But she knew the past with Black Ice. "Boy, I'm telling you the devil is coming for you. You don't have to believe me, but I have something for you and Envy." Rachel hit a switch and a secret door opened to reveal arsenal of guns.

"Damn mom, I thought you was all holy and stuff?" Michael stated.

"Boy shut up. I am and you never doubt that. I'm just ready for the devil when he comes."

Envy and Michael stood there in shock looking at all the guns. They were more surprised than anything. Michael always knew his mother was a fighter and knew that's where he got it from. Rachel pulled out two melt cases and opened one to reveal two chrome 50 caliber desert eagle handguns with holsters. "Damn mom, where you get those? There beautiful."

"Don't worry about that, baby, but they're yours and one of the most powerful handguns in the world. There 50 caliber and the clips are extended so you get 22 bullets in each one. Michael picked up the guns. He had seen a lot of guns in his short life, but never none like these and so pretty. Then he noticed the handles were pearl and there was word writing on the side of them that read, 'The right hand of God.' "This is for you, Envy," Rachel said while opening up the next melt case. Inside were twin forty caliber handguns. They were the same in every way as Michael's guns with two things different: the handle was pink and pearl and the guns were smaller. "Envy baby, I don't know how you feel about guns. I really don't like them myself, but you must be a strong woman being with my son."

"Guns don't bother me, Rachel. I'm from Brooklyn. I know how to use them but never thought I had too."

"Girl, if you call me Rachel one more time."

"Ok mom," Envy said with a smile on her face.

"I got one more than for you Envy. This is a 3.57 sub nose magnum with strap holsters. You put this on your thigh under your jeans or dress. I know how much you love you some fashion and I don't want you to mess up none of your pretty outfits, but I don't want you trying to carry the other two around, but Envy I want you to carry this all the time. I see it in my dreams you need this child."

"Mom, we're going to be okay. You need to stop this you're just having bad dreams."

"Michael, I am not going to keep telling you. God shown me signs in my dreams. I'll pray for you two."

Michael looked at his mother then kissed her on her forehead and grabbed the two melt cases.

"Boy, listen to me the devil is coming. Be

ready and watch out for that boy. There's something about him."

"With that note we're leaving. Envy, come on. Love you, mom," Michael said as he walked up the basement stairs and seen Mike talking to Janet and laughing. "Come on Mike, we're going home now."

"Okay," Mike replied and said bye to Janet as they made their way to the car.

On the ride home Envy had so many questions she wanted to ask Michael, but knew it wasn't the time. As they pulled up in front of their brownstone house on Gates Avenue in Brooklyn, they saw a brown skin woman in a gray suit standing there. "That's Ms. Green. She's going to take me anyway!" Mike yelled and was looking around for ways to escape.

"No Mike, I spoke to her this morning. She said you can stay, but she has to check out our house to make sure it's safe and sit and talk with us. That's all Mike," Envy stated.

"You swear," Mike replied.

"Yes baby, that's all."

The three of them got out of the car. Michael and Envy began to unload all the bags from the trunk. "Hey Ms. Green, nice to meet you. I'm Envy Kartel and this is Michael Ice, Jr. We spoke earlier."

"Yes, nice to meet you to Miss Kartel."

"Oh just call me Envy, Ms. Green. Come on in," Envy replied as they walked into the house and Mike followed nervously and scared that he would be taken away.

"I'll put up the bags," Michael stated. Envy sat down on the couch and Ms. Green did the same.

"Okay, from your files I see you go to school for fashion and work with mental patients and that Michael Ice, Jr. is the owner of the community center in Brownsville that also gets funded by the state."

"Yes Ms. Green, you have everything right. Okay, so Mike can stay here. You and Michael have to sign some paper and finish showing me around."

"Not a problem Ms. Green." Envy took Ms. Green around the house and she was more than impressed. The house was decorated with the best things money could buy.

"Who decorated the house?" Ms. Green asked.

"Please girl, you know it was me. It takes a man to buy a house, but a woman to make it a home." Envy replied.

"I hear that girl. I love your place. You have great taste. Now all I need is for you and Michael to sign here." Ms. Green said as she pulled out some papers. Michael came down the stairs and signed the papers. "Ok Michael and Envy, we're all done. I have to come by once a month to visit the house and I'll bring you the rest of the paper work you need on Mike."

"Ok Ms. Green it was nice meeting you and we look forward to your next visit." Michael said while shaking her hand.

"Bye Envy and girl you have to take me

shopping with you one day or help me pick out nice things for my place."

"I got you, Ms. Green. You have a good day," Envy replied.

"I guess everything went our way baby," Michael said while wrapping his arms around Envy.

"You should have known it would. We make a great team in and everyone loves you and loves my fashion style."

"Yea they do baby." Michael replied while slowly kissing her lips and making her wet as each kiss was deeper than the last. There tongue danced in each other's mouth.

Mike walked into the living room. "So am I staying?" Mike asked causing Envy and Michael to break their embrace.

"See we can't be doing that now. We have a child around," Envy said walking away very seductively.

"Damn something about a woman in heels is so sexy," Michael said out loud to himself. "Yea, you're going to stay Mike. We worked everything out. You'll be with me and Miss Envy for now on and we're going to take good care of you."

"Really?" Mike said with a cheesy smile on his face.

"Yes really, now go try on some of those new clothes Envy picked out for you."

The door bell rang and Michael walked to it, "Who is it?"

"It's Detective Roy and Tommy. May we speak with Michael?" Michael opened up the door. "Are you Michael Ice, Jr.?" a short white detective asked. He had on a grey suit and had blond hair and next to him was his partner who was overweight with black hair.

"Yes, I am sir. What is this about?" Michael asked.

"May we come in, sir?"

"Yes, come in," Michael replied and led them to the living room where they all sat down.

"Okay Michael, like I said, I'm detective Roy and this is my partner, Detective Tommy. I have to ask you a few things. Where were you last night around 9pm?

"I was home with my girl. Why?" Michael replied.

"There was a shootout in the parking lot of the project in Brownsville right next to the community center that you own. Do you know anything about it?

"No, Detective Roy, I don't," Michael replied.

"Listen, Michael or Evil, yes I know what they call you on the streets." Detective Roy said with a smirk on his face. "I know who your father is, Black Ice. My father spent his whole career chasing him and lost his partner just like you, Michael or Evil. I am a junior my father was Detective Roy, Sr. and my father wasn't able to get your father, but I will and if I can't fucking get him, I'll get you. There have been bodies in the last ten years popping up with missing body parts -- your father's style, but I don't think it's him. I believe it was you."

"It sounds like you have a problem,

Detective Roy. I'm not like my father and if you feel like you must follow your father's footsteps go ahead, asshole. I work with the state and have friends in high places and more than the Chief of Police, who will love how you been questioning me, someone who's trying to better the community and slow down the drug rate in Brooklyn." Michael stated with his devilish grin on his face.

"You're just like him. I'll fucking prove it somehow and will put your ass away behind bars where you belong just like your father," Detective Roy shouted.

"I think you need to leave my house, now," Michael replied.

Detective Roy and Tommy got up and left. "We will be seeing you again." Detective Roy said as he walked out the door.

"And you will be losing your job," Michael stated then laughed and shut the door.

Detective Roy and Tommy jumped into the car. "I know he knows something, Tommy. And it's a matter of time before we get him."

"I hope your right, Roy, because he does know people in high places. I seen the pictures of him with the police chief even the DA."

"Fuck that black, mother fucker, I doubt they do anything to help him and did you see how nice the inside of his house was? We work hard and we're still not living that good," Detective Roy replied.

"But Roy, he does help women and children."

"I don't care. Do you like him or

something, Tommy?"

"No Roy, I'm just stating the fact."

"I don't want to hear the facts. He's a monster that's all there is to it," Detective Roy said as he drove off.

Michael dialed a number and the person picked up on the first ring. "Hey Michael, what's going on? What can I do for you?"

"I have an issue. It's a Detective Roy. I think he's going to be a problem for me."

"Oh don't worry, Michael, I'll take care of it."

"Thank you," Michael replied and hung up.

"I'm about to cook," Envy said as she walked in, "Who was you talking to baby?" she asked.

"I'll tell you all about it. So, can me and Mike help you cook?" Michael replied.

"Sure why not?"

Chapter 10

Pooky lay on the bed still in pain. He now had a bag strapped to his thigh. There was tube in it that was connected to his bladder for him to urine in. He felt his ear and noticed for the first time a big piece was cut off the top of it. "Shit not only am I deaf in that ear, it's also cut up. I'm going to kill Evil and that little fucking boy!!" Pooky yelled out in anger as the older man with long dreads walked into the room and looked at him lying on the bed. "I messed up man. I almost had him if it wasn't for that little boy."

"Don't worry, Pooky. We will get another chance and we will kill off them both," the older man replied, "By the way, why do you want Evil dead?"

"I have my reasons, but you never told me yours. You just came to me with a plan to kill him and I was down with it. I hated him for years."

Ceaser looked back down at Pooky, "It's not Evil I want. It's Black Ice. I hope you kill Evil and you help me kill Black Ice. Ten years ago, I worked for Black Ice and he took everything from my woman, Roxy, my son, and my place in this world and he thought he took my life." Ceaser said as his mind flashed back to him sitting in that tight, dark barrel with his son's head and arms on his lap as he sunk to the bottom of Coney Island Ocean. "And I would have died if it wasn't for the police in a boat in the middle of the ocean that seen Black Ice dump the barrel in the ocean. When they sent four divers to get the barrel not knowing what was inside and was shocked when they opened it and found me halfway dead, passed out, and covered in my son's blood and body parts. I kept on living in hiding for ten years. I've been waiting for the day to get my chance to have my revenge on Black Ice, but he hasn't shown his face yet. And with all the kidnapping and more crack heads popping up in Brooklyn, I just know it's him behind it. Somehow and when we kill Evil he will show his face and will be next. The sins of the father will be paid by the son," Ceaser stated as him and Pooky both smiled as they thought of Evil and Black Ice dying.

Tiffany looked at Black Ice go to the steel door and punch in the code. The door popped open and he walked out and it shut behind him. She knew it was Friday and Black Ice was having a meeting with his henchman and also to go out and grab more women and girls from off the street. 'This is my night I can feel it. I know I can pull it off and get away,' she thought to herself as she quickly jumped out of the bed and stumbled a little. Her legs were weak and her pussy was sore from the beating Black Ice did to it. She made her way to the shower and hopped in and washed up as fast as she could and put on an all black sweat suit. I'll wait for an hour until I feel him and his henchmen are out.

Across town in Brownville Brooklyn, two black vans pulled up on a dark block on Howard Avenue. Four men dressed in black jumped out of both vans than opened the back door in each van. There were six women wearing only white dirty T-shirts and looked to be only eighty pounds each, scared, and shaking for their life. A few of the girls had fat stomachs, not from being pregnant. The first henchmen spoke, "Listen, you remember what you've been told if any of you say a word about what happened to you or where you have been. We will find you and if you think the last few months of your fucking life have been hell, you don't know what the fuck we will do next to you. Now get the hell out of here. You're free," the henchmen yelled while the other guys grabbed the women and pulled them out of the van then handed them each crack the size of an eight ball. The women looked around with fear then slowly walked off like zombies. Some sat right there on the sidewalk and pulled out there crack pipe, filled it up, and began to smoke. Black Ice smirked and was more than pleased as the vans pulled off.

Two women got off the train from work and were heading home. Two men jumped out of a black van and grabbed them from behind and pressed knives to their throats. They screamed and kicked, but it was no use as the strong men tossed them in to the back of the van crying.

Three sixteen year old girls were leaving from a party then were knocked out with small baseball bat and dragged into the van.

Tiffany's instincts told her it was now or never. She knew Black Ice and most of his men will be out in the street kidnapping more women or making drugs sales. She walked to the door and punched in the code 5, 17, 32, 7. "Yes I got it right," she said out loud as the door opened and she looked both ways sticking her head out of the door making sure there were no guards there. She crept down the hallway making sure to stay close to the wall so the cameras wouldn't see her. She stepped into the elevator and pressed the button for the basement. Once in the basement, she slowly headed down the hall to the third big steel door. In her heart she knew there were a few guards around, but she couldn't leave without Star and Yasmin. There were no henchmen guarding the big steel door to the room where all the other women were kept. She knew it wouldn't be because all the men were getting a new women or fresh meat as Black Ice would tell her. She punched in the code she seen Black Ice use. The door popped open a cloud of white smoke rushed out and hit her face. "Shit, what the fuck am I doing?" she said out loud as the crack called to her and made her want to smoke. She walked into a large room and had to wait until her eyes adjusted to the darkness. She looked around and saw there were only a few women chained to the wall. "Good that means Black Ice and his men are setting some of the women free, but kidnapping more," she said to herself as she used her hand to fan some of the smoke out of her face. She could see her best friend sitting on the floor rocking back and forth. "Star, it's me!" Tiffany said bending down next to her.

Star stopped rocking and looked up at Tiffany. "I did what you said and stopped smoking until you came, but the voices in my head kept telling me to smoke and my body hurts and calls for the crack. I didn't know how long I could fight it."

"Me too, Star. It's the same for me, but we

have to fight so we can get a way. You must have a clear head. Where's Yasmin?" Tiffany asked as soon as she asked the question moaning could be heard. Star pointed her finger to the dark corner where a henchman was pounding in and out of Yasmin. "Can your chains reach over there into that corner? I have a plan," Tiffany stated.

"Yea, it can reach," Star replied.

Tiffany and Star both got up without making a sound and walked slowly and quietly over to the henchmen that was still so deep in Yasmin's sweet wet box. He never noticed them. "We have to kill him Star. It's the only way," Tiffany whispered as her and Star threw the chain that was around her ankle around the henchman's neck.

"Oh shit!" He tried to yell as Star and Tiffany both pulled on the chain and put their knees pressed into his back.

"Pull, Star pull!!!" Tiffany yelled as the henchman gasped for air as he tried to pull the chain off his neck. His eyes rolled back into his head and a loud snapping noise was heard as his neck broke.

"Oh my God, we broke his neck," Star said as she and Tiffany let go of the chain and his body fell on top of Yasmin.

"Get him off of me!"Yasmin yelled as she pushed his body to the side and his dick slid out of her. She lay there the whole time just watching them choking him.

"Hurry Star," said as Tiffany started to dig in the henchman's pocket and found a key in on his shoulder holster. She pulled out his heckler 9mm handgun. "Give me a leg," she ordered. Star leaned her feet towards her and she unlocked the chain. "Now, you Yasmin," Yasmin did the same.

"What about the other girls?" Star asked.

"Listen, we don't have time to free them all only free two. The rest we have to leave. I'm sorry we'll come back with the police to help them."

"Okay," Star said as she unlocked two girls, "Come on follow us," she said to the two women she set free.

The other women in the room began to cry and scream, "Free us, free us please! Please, don't leave us!"

"We will be back for you I swear," Tiffany yelled back as she crept out the steel door with the heckler 9mm in her hand. Star, Yasmin and the other two women followed quickly making their way down the hallway. They got into the elevator and pressed floor one. They got off on the first floor.

"Which way is it Tiffany?" Star asked.

"I don't know. I'm trying to remember, but there are too many doors," Tiffany replied as all four of the women crept down the long hallway. Men voices could be heard coming from behind a steel door, "Sshhhh," Tiffany said as she put her finger to her lips, "Be quiet. One of these doors goes to the parking lot of this warehouse. I remember that's the way they dragged us in here, but I can't recall the door."

"I know which one," Yasmin said speaking for the first time, "Follow me."

"Okay," Tiffany replied as she followed her with the other women.

"It's this door here!" Yasmin said pointing to a big black steel door.

"I think I know the code to open it, but you have to go out first, Tiffany, because you have the gun," Yasmin stated.

"Okay, just move faster," Tiffany replied while looking up and down the hallway scared their going to be spotted. Yasmin punched the code in the keypad and the door creaked open. Tiffany's instincts and whole body told her something was wrong as she walked through the door with the gun aimed into the darkness as the other women followed. "Yasmin, I think this was the wrong door," Tiffany said as she walked into what looked like a dark room, but couldn't tell because there were no light.

Yasmin watched all four women walk deeper in as she stood outside of the door. "I know it was," Yasmin yelled then laughed as she pushed the door a shut.

"What the fuck!" Star and Tiffany yelled as they turn around to see their friend locked them in. Tiffany ran back to the door and tried to push it open.

"Get it open! Get it open! Hurry!" Star and the other women yelled.

"I can't I'm trying the code call, but the door won't open up," Tiffany said.

"Why would Yasmin lock us in here? She's one of our best friends in the world?" Star asked while looking over Tiffany's back as she tried to punch in the code.

Then laughter could be heard in the dark.

All four women stopped and turned around. The room was pitch black. They barely could see their hands in front of their face. “What! What was that?” one of the women asked.

“Shhhh, be quiet. I don’t know, but it don’t sound right,” Tiffany replied. The laughter got louder and footsteps could be heard getting closer and closer.

“What the fuck is that?” Star yelled as fear ran through her body and the other women as well as the laughter went on hysterically.

“It don’t sound human,” Tiffany said as she pointed the gun into the darkness as the footsteps and laughter got louder and closer. The four women looked down at twelve pair of glowing eyes.

“What the hell?” one of the women screamed then something grabbed her leg and locked on to it, “Help! Help! Help, please, ahhhhhh!” she screamed as she was dragged into the darkness. “Ahhhh, oh god! Oh god! Ahhh!” she screamed louder and louder and sounds of her flesh could be heard being ripped and torn apart and bones cracking. What sounded like something eating her alive. “Help!!” she screamed then all that could be heard was her choking on her own blood.

“Oh lord, what the hell is that? I can’t see her,” the other women screamed along with Star.

“I think there dogs,” Tiffany said while pointing the gun into the darkness.

“Shit, those are not dogs. That shit was fucking laughing. Dogs do not fucking laugh, Tiffany.”

“I don’t know what they are, but they look

like dogs," Tiffany yelled just as the glowing eyes looked their way and started to run towards them.

"Oh shit! Their coming," Star yelled.

Tiffany aimed at their eyes. The only thing she could see clear and began to pull the trigger of the heckler 9mm. Boom! Boom! Boom! The sound of gun fire echoed through the air as one of the dog like creatures flew in the air to bite Star. A bullet hit it between the eyes killing it and sent it flying backwards. Tiffany continued to shoot. Bullets crashed into two of the dog like creatures killing them. Then one got close enough to bite and lock on to one of the other girl's leg that had escaped with them, "Ahhh help! Help!" she screamed as Tiffany aimed and shot it in the side causing it to release its grip and hollered in pain and died while the other creatures retreated into the darkness. Their laugh echoed through the room.

"You shot my pets, bitch!" was the last thing Tiffany heard from Black Ice voice as something hit her on the back of her head and she lost consciousness.

Star and the other women screamed as Black Ice hit both of them in the head with a small metal baseball bat knocking them out.

Two hours later, Tiffany woke up to the sounds of moaning. She focused her eyes and couldn't believe what she was seeing. Her friend, Yasmin, was on her knees licking the tip of Black Ice's dick then pushed it all the way in her mouth as he held the back of her head and fucked her mouth like it was pussy and let out a loud moan as he busted all in her mouth. Yasmin stuck her tongue out to show him the cum then moaned, "Mmmmm!!" as she swallowed it.

Tiffany tried to move then realized her hands were chained up on the wall above her head and her feet were chained as well. She looked over to see that Star and the other women that were with them were chained to the wall also. Their eyes were opened, but they were too scared to speak or move.

"Get off of me now, bitch," Black Ice yelled as he pulled up his jeans and threw in an eight ball of crack onto the floor. Yasmin quickly grabbed the ball and broke a little piece off and stuffed it into her glass pipe and held the lighter at the end of it and inhaled the white thick smoke. "So, you're finally awake, Tiffany?" Black Ice asked as he walked towards her with a metal baseball bat in one hand and a cigarette mixed with crack in the other he inhaled and let out the smoke out from his nose. He now stood face to face with her. "So, you thought you could escape me, bitch? What did I tell you! I said no one ever gets away from me and if they do they will pay! Ha ha ha!" Black Ice let out his sinister laugh and swung the bat hitting her in the knee.

"Ahhhh!" she cried out in pain.

"Bitch, I told you to never run and you killed four of my pets!" he yelled as he swung again hitting her in the thigh so hard she screamed and cried as tears ran down her face. She felt like she wanted to pass out from the pain. He then walked to Star and the other woman and hit them both repeatedly in the legs and thighs with the bat. The women cried and screamed and tried to wiggle away, but it was in vain with their hands chained up over their heads and feet chained to the wall they couldn't move.

"Yasmin, why? Why you betray us?" Tiffany yelled out with tears in her voice.

Yasmin was sitting on the floor and looked up from smoking on her crack pipe. "I'm sorry, Tiffany and Star. I couldn't help it. He said I'll be set free and have all the crack I could want. We had no chance of ever getting free, unless he let us go. He would've caught us anyway. So, I might as well take care myself first."

"You bitch we grew up together and were best friends me, you, Tiffany, and Jesse. How could you cross us?" Star cried out while Black Ice beat her.

Yasmin inhaled more smoke from the crack pipe as she thought of her best friend Jesse that Black Ice killed on their first night in this hell hole a tear ran down her face as she lowered her head out of shame.

"She's fucked and just the way I want her," Black Ice said laughing as he walked back to Tiffany. "You still have to pay for killing my four pets. See I talked to your friend, Yasmin, and knew your ass would try to escape one day and told her to lead you to this room with my pets in. She really thought I was going to set her ass free. Haahaaaa!" Black Ice said and busted out laughing.

"But you promised me you set me free," Yasmin replied looking up at Black Ice.

He walked over to her and back hand

smacked her. She screamed. "I'll set you free if I fucking want to now shut the fuck up." Yasmin laid there on the floor crying. "Now back to you, Tiffany, for killing my pets. What I'm going to do to you? Hmmm," Black Ice looked at the three women chained to wall and whistled. Out of the corner of the room, three doglike creatures came out and walked toward them. Their mouths were covered in blood. Their fur was striped and brown and their front legs were longer than there back legs. Tiffany looked and knew she had seen these animals somewhere. Then they started to laugh as Black Ice bent down and pet them.

"Hyenas! That's what they are, but how are they in the city? They live in Africa or South America," Tiffany yelled out with shock.

"Yes, you're right," Black Ice replied with his devilish grin on his face. "They're hyenas. My pets I paid a lot of money for them. There a myth that I found out is true that they have the strongest bite and jaws than any other animal in the world. They can even crack bones with their teeth and eat it. See that blood spot over there?" Black Ice said and pointed to a big spot of blood, "That used to be that other girl that tried to escape with you. See there isn't even a bone left just blood. They even ate the other four dead hyenas you killed, Tiffany. So, their full, but very greedy," Black Ice said as he stood up and looked at Yasmin on the floor who was scared to death to move. He grabbed her hand. "Wait, what are you doing? You promised not to hurt me."

"Didn't I tell you to shut up bitch?" Black

Ice yelled as he chained her hands and feet to the wall. "How can I trust you to go free when you betrayed your own best friends for some crack and the dream of freedom? Hell fucking no! As soon as I let you go, you will tell the cops what has happened to you these last few months and I can't have that. The only reason women get to go free from here is because they keep their mouths shut and continue to smoke crack making my business grow." Black Ice laughed and so did the hyenas. "Shut up!" he yelled and the hyenas got quiet and lowered their heads.

Tiffany noticed that even those beasts that can chew a person's bones and eat it had fear when it came to Black Ice. That even they can even sense his evil as if he was the devil himself. Black Ice walked to Tiffany and rubbed her stomach then looked at the other three women. They were all skinny and had lost a lot of weight, but he could still tell that all of them were pregnant.

"Tiffany, I like you, but you try to escape and you killed my pets. These hyenas are stripped and rare hyenas. I raised them myself and paid a lot of fucking money to get them. More than your life is worth. So, here's the deal. In order for you to live, you better do whatever I tell you to. Do you understand me?"

"Yes, I do," Tiffany answered her whole body shaking with fear not knowing what he would do next.

Black Ice pulled out a box cutter from his back pocket. He looked at Tiffany then walked slowly and looked at Star up and down and then the other woman that tried to escape with them then Yasmin. He looked at the women who tried to escape with them once more from head to toe. "What's your name?" he asked.

"My…my name is Kim," she answered scared to death.

"Well Kim, it's not your lucky night. You shouldn't have tried to escape with these three bitches. Now, you have to pay," Black Ice said as he raised the box cutter to her face.

"Noooo... no! Please, I'm sorry. I'm sorry!" she screamed out and tried to wiggle away, but her hands were chained above her head to the wall with her feet. Black Ice grabbed her chin and began to cut deep on her face. First, he cut a deep line on her forehead near her hairline. "Ahhhhh!Ahhhh!" she screamed in agonizing pain as he held onto her face and cut deep lines all around it until he cut under her chin. He dropped the box cutter and looked at his work. "Please no! Please, no more, stop!" Kim begged and cried not knowing her words and pleas were going on a deaf ear and a cold heart. He then stuck his finger nails into the long cut he made on her forehead by her hairline and pulled. "Ahhhh!" Kim screamed as loud as she could as she felt her skin being ripped from her face. He ripped most of it off from her forehead then stopped leaving a big piece of skin hanging to her eyebrows. "Hahaha!" his devilish laugh echoed through the room as he walked back to Tiffany.

Tiffany, Star, and Yasmin watched in horror and were screaming and crying out of fear. They have never seen anything so gruesome in their life.

"You're the devil!" Tiffany said as he stood in front of her face.

"Yes, I fucking am."

Kim's screams and cries were so loud Tiffany wanted to close her eyes and try to block it out, but the laughter from the hyenas that were sitting near kept her from doing so.

"Now, Tiffany, remember what I fucking told you. If you want to live, do what I say."

"Yes, I'll do anything just don't hurt me." Tiffany replied with tears in her voice as Black Ice uncuffed her hands and her feet. He grabbed her by the hair and dragged her in front of Kim who was crying in pain as the flesh on her face hung and blood was dripping down her white T-shirt that was now red from being soaked in blood.

"Now, Tiffany, grab the hanging piece of her skin on her face and I want you to pull down until you rip all the flesh off her face."

"What? What you want me to do? I can't do that." Tiffany replied while looking at Kim. Kim looked up at her and Black Ice.

"Please! Please, no more. I won't run no more. I promise."

"Tiffany, you fucking do it and you do it now or else," Black Ice yelled. You think you really have a choice? If you don't do it, I'll kill your friends first, very slowly. I know you don't care about this one," he said pointing to Yasmin. "But I know, you love this one," he said as he pointed to Star. "Then I'll kill you. Don't think I won't because you're carrying my child because I fucking will! The only reason you get better treatment is because you look like Roxy, but I already let you know, I killed Roxy when she ran and she was pregnant with my child. So, don't think I won't do the same to your ass." Black Ice said then grinned. Tiffany now knew he was the devil. "Now, you have one second to pull off the flesh on her face or I'll let my pets here make a meal out of all of you."

Tiffany looked at Star and her stomach than Kim as tears ran down her face. "I'm sorry, Kim."

"No, please don't!"

Tiffany took both hands and grabbed the hanging piece of skin and dug her nails into it like she had seen Black Ice do. "Ahhhh!" Kim screamed in pain as Tiffany pulled down.

"I'm sorry. I'm sorry," Tiffany yelled as she continued to pull down. The sound of the skin ripping and tearing made Tiffany stop. Star and Yasmin looked on in fear and was crying the whole time.

"Stop, please stop!" Kim cried out. Tiffany slowly started pulling down and didn't want to continue. She looked back at Black Ice who was staring with his evil look letting her know she'd better finish. Tiffany closed her eyes and pulled down fast and hard with all her might. Kim let out one loud scream and passed out from the pain. Tiffany opened her eyes and couldn't believe what she saw. The flesh from Kim's face had been ripped all the way off. All that was left was muscle and blood. Tiffany looked at her hand and dropped the large piece of flesh that was in her grasp. She bent over and began to throw up.

Black Ice laughed as he picked up the flesh off the floor. "This will go good with my collection. You did good, Tiffany." He grabbed her by the arm and cuffed her to the wall.

"Look at what you made me do! Look at what you made me do!" she screamed and began to cry along with Star and Yasmin.

Black Ice looked at her then walked to Kim who was still passed out. He uncuffed her hands and feet and she fell face first. "She's no good. No more than just dead meat with her face looking like that now. Get her!" Black Ice screamed and for the first time since he told the hyenas to sit. They moved and the hyena's laughter echoed through the room as they rushed Kim's body. The first hyena bit into Kim's head with his large mouth wide open and was able to fit most of her head in his mouth. Kim woke up from the pain and let out a blood crawling scream as the hyenas strong jaw crushed her head and bones and her brains oozed out in to its mouth. As the rest of the hyenas attacked her body, ripping pieces of flesh from it from left and right and fighting each other over pieces of meat that used to be Kim's body.

Tiffany, Star, and Yasmin screamed and cried in horror and were unable to move because of the chains and just had to watch. Black Ice pulled out his crack pipe and filled the tip of it with crack and began to smoke and inhaled deeply while watching his hyenas feed. "Greedy motherfucker, all they do is kill, shit, and eat." he said out loud.

Tiffany stopped crying long enough to look

at Black Ice. "I'll kill you. I swear I'll find away to kill the devil," she said in her head as she stopped crying and her heart turn cold.

Outside the room two henchmen, named Jason and Tiwan guarded the door. "Damn that nigga Black Ice is crazy," Jason said as he heard the women screaming and crying and the laughter of the hyenas.

"Yo, don't say that shit out loud," Tiwan replied.

"It's my mouth so fuck it. I can't help but to think and wonder how a fucking crack head comes up with the plan of grabbing women and turning them into crack heads and have all the drug dealers buy weight of crack from him. He's a fucking crack head."

Tiwan looked at Jason. "Didn't I tell you to shut the fuck up? You know the stories and rumors of Black Ice. He's not normal he's the devil in the flesh. You know the last two fools that talked bad about him and crossed him that worked for him what happened to them right? He killed ones whole family and the other he chopped his son up and threw him in a barrel into the ocean with his son's head and body parts," Tiwan replied.

"Word I heard you, but I'm not scared of him no matter how bad he is. He's just a super crack head and bleeds just like us. I think we can take over this shit and kill him." Jason said with a smile on his face. He turned his head to look at Tiwan in the eyes to see if he was down with his plan, but to only see chrome Uzi pointed at his face.

"Fool, I told to shut up. I'm not going to die

with you or worse get my whole family chopped up. We damn near rich and get to fuck all these pretty ass women when they first come in here and get them cracked out. You can't leave well enough alone? So you're done," Tiwan stated as he squeezed the trigger of the Uzi and a hail of bullets ripped through Jason's face and body. He slumped over dead. "I told you to shut up," Tiwan said looking at Jason's dead body on the floor all tore up by bullets.

Black Ice stepped out of the room. "What the fuck is going on out here? What's the shooting about, Tiwan?"

"It was nothing boss, just another fool getting ideas," Tiwan replied.

"I like you, Tiwan, you're no fool. Now drag his body into the room for the hyenas to eat later. I know they should be full by now," he said as he walked down the hallway smoking a cigarette mixed with crack.

Chapter 11

Envy was the first one up for the day in the house and spent the morning cleaning. She went to the mailbox and was happy when she opened it. There was a yellow big envelope from ACS. That only meant one thing that this must be Mike's paperwork his birth certificate and social security card. She went back inside and sat down at the kitchen table and opened the envelope. She began to look through the paperwork. She stopped when she got to the death certificate and report of Mike's mother. Envy's mouth dropped as she continued to read and couldn't believe her eyes. "This shit can't be! How in the world could it be? This is crazy," she said out loud while reading out loud. Mike's real name is Michael Jazzer. An ACS worker let him go by Mike because it's the only name he responded to and his mother was Roxy Jazzer. In the police report, it said she died from a gunshot wound to the head, not at giving birth to Mike, like he was told. And the killer was Black Ice also the child's father proven by a D.N.A test by one of the cigarette buds he had smoked and left behind on a crime scene. Envy's jaw dropped. "Wow, how the hell am I going to tell Michael that Mike is really his brother and that's the real reason why they look alike, got the same cold eyes, and blank stare." Envy quickly put everything back into the envelope then put it in to her purse.

Mike sat in his new room on his bed looking around. He never felt so happy. Everything he could want was here. Michael and Envy was to be his new family and his own room and bed to sleep on. He couldn't remember the last time he had his own bed. He sat on the edge of the bed with a clear jar filled with water inside of it floating around was a piece of Pooky's ear that he cut off a few days ago. He looked at it float around and smiled.

Michael walked inside Mike's room. "Hey, you want to come to the center with me today maybe you can play with some of the other kids while I get some work done? And then me and you can play a game of basketball."

The sound of Michael's voice scared Mike and he swiftly put the jar he was holding up under the pillow. "Yea, I haven't been to the center in a while. I want to come," Mike replied.

"Uhmm, what was you just hiding, Mike?"

"Oh, it was nothing."

"I'll be ready to go soon. Ok?" Michael said and raised his right eyebrow wondering what he just saw Mike push up under the pillow.

Michael left the room and shut the door behind him. As soon as he did, Mike took the jar from up under the pillow and put it under the bed. Michael walked into his bedroom and went to the bathroom that was built into the room. He got undressed and jumped into the shower. He let the hot water hit his body as he thought about his father. 'I know you will come for me, but when? I'm ready for you and been waiting,' he said out loud.

Envy walked into the bedroom and heard the water running in the shower. 'How in the world am I going to tell him that Mike is really his brother from the woman his father cheated on his mother with?' Envy shook her head as she made her way to the bathroom. She couldn't see him clearly through the shower curtain, but could see the frame of his body and just the sight of it, made her pussy wet. She began to rub her clit through her jeans and let out a soft moan.

Michael slid the curtain aside to see her standing there with lust in her eyes and her hand now in her pants rubbing her clit. When their eyes met, there was love and passion in the air. Envy removed her clothes slowly. This was only teasing Michael more as he watched her voluptuous body and her caramel skin complexion that seemed to glow. She stepped into the shower. "Ooow!" she moaned as the warm water hit her back and rippled around her skin.

"Damn baby, you sexy." Michael said as he held her close and they kissed passionately and deeply. Their tongues danced in each other's mouths. Envy reached down and grabbed his nine inch, hard dick into her hands and jerked it back and forth with long, slow strokes, loving the way it felt. Michael pulled away and got on his knees. Envy leaned back as he took her clit into his mouth. "Shit," she moaned as the sweet sensation of his lips sent chills through her body. The water hit her face and hair and ran down her body and onto Michaels as he licked her clit up and down.

"Shit, yes baby, yes. Suck that shit. Suck it, boo," she moaned. Michael took her pussy lips into his mouth and then her clit and sucked it real fast driving Envy even more wild. She rubbed her breast and let her hands roam her body. “Damn, fuck Daddy,” she moaned.

“You like that, baby? You going to cum for me all in my mouth?” Michael moaned in between sucking her pussy.

“Ohh shit, yes daddy! Mmm, I love it.” Envy moaned even louder as she felt her nut building up while her body jerked back and forth.

Michael knew what time it was. He grabbed both her ass cheeks and pushed his face deeper into her sweet box and he licked even faster and sucked even harder. “Mmmmm, oh shit, oh shit! I’m about to cum, damn daddy!” Envy screamed. He licked her clit so fast her legs began to tremble. “Damn, I’m cumming! I’m cumming!” Envy screamed.

Michael held on for dear life as her body buckled and she came harder than she ever did before in her life. Michael took one more suck of her sweet juices to saver the sweet taste. He stood up and kissed her. “You see how sweet you taste?” Envy shook her head while licking her lips.

“Damn, you know I hate when you hold me like that when I’m cumming. That shit is so sensitive and be having my ass shaking,” Envy said while smiling. Their lips met as he lifted her up in his arms and slid his dick inside of her. She bit her bottom lip.

“Shit,” Michael groaned as he felt the wetness of her walls. He pumped long and hard making her pussy slide up and down his dick while he was holding her by her thick thighs.

“Shit! Fuck!” Envy yelled as his dick filled

her inside. Her nails dug into his back as each stroke teased and pleased her. "Fuck me! Fuck me like that, damn daddy." Her eyes rolled towards the back of her head as she came all over his big black dick.

Michael carefully put her down and turned her around as she held the shower walls and arched her back. Michael slid his dick inside and wasted no time to pound on her pussy. He thrusted his body in and out as hard as he could feeling deeper and deeper inside. He smacked her ass and grabbed her wet hair and pulled on it while stuffing his dick deeper in.

"Oh shit baby, it feels so good," Envy screamed as water splashed everywhere. "Damn daddy!" Envy yelled as loud as she could as she came again. Michael pounded hard and then slowed down with long strokes.

"Shit baby, that pussy is sweet," he groaned as he nutted and emptied himself inside of her.

Something caught the corner of his eyes. He turned to look and saw Mike standing at the bathroom door. "Oh shit! You shouldn't be in here," he yelled as he quickly covered Envy with his body.

Mike stood there with a blank stare and walked in deeper and for the first time Michael and Envy both noticed a man standing behind him with a gun pointed to his head. "Shit!" Envy yelled realizing they both been caught off guard. Another man walked into the room and now had his gun aimed at Envy and Michael and was standing next to his partner.

"What the fuck you two want?" Michael said with a smirk on his face.

The two men looked at each other and laughed. "Pooky and Ceaser sent us to finish the job and kill your ass. And you need to wipe that smile off your face or we'll do it for you. We were told that if we get the drop on you, to kill your punk ass fast because you supposed to be some evil, bad ass killer or something."

"He don't look like no evil bad ass killer to me," the other gunmen said then laughed.

"Yea, you're right. He just some young punk caught with his dick out," both gunmen busted out laughing.

Michael looked at Envy who was standing naked next to him. On the shower wall that was next to her, Michael had made a hook that held two 9 mm rugers that were made of plastic with silencers on them. When he first put them there, Envy had asked him why and if they hang them in the shower won't they get wet and rusty then won't work. But Michael had explained to her that the guns were the new 9 mm Rugers that cops use and being made of plastic they wouldn't rust, the only thing metal were the bullets. Envy mind raced to everything he told her. She remembered him telling her that this house was his father's and that he left it to him. So, that means if we stayed there, one day Black Ice will come for him, but they'd be ready. He hid guns all around the house, in the shower, up under the bed and pillow, in the kitchen, even behind the toilet. He told her that no one would catch them. Envy had laughed when he first told her that, but as she snapped back to reality it all became clear to her.

Envy looked at the two gunmen and was scared, but not for her life, but for Mike and Michael. She knew the gunmen couldn't see the 9 mm Ruger's, unless they were standing in the shower.

"Yo, you're still fucking smirking ass hole! You think this situation is funny? I'm going to fuck your girl in front of you then kill her and the kid and save you for last." As the gunmen walked toward Envy and Michael, Michael gave Mike a look he seen before on that night in the Brownsville parking lot and he knew what to do.

Mike dropped to the floor as fast as he could. The two gunmen looked down at him and were shocked by his actions. Envy knew she had no time to waste in one swift move she grabbed both the guns and tossed one to Michael. Before Michael could catch his gun, Envy aimed and fired two shots. The first hollow point bullet went through the gunmen's neck and the next one through his chest. He grabbed his neck and stumbled backwards. The next gunmen looked up from the floor to stop staring at Mike to only see blood gushing and pouring out of his friend and him stumbling backwards until he hit the wall and slid down it with his hand on his neck.

"What the fuck happened?" he yelled and turned his head to face Michael and Envy as soon as he did Michael squeezed the trigger four times. The bullets flew out of the gun without making a sound because of the silencers and left four large holes in the gunmen's head. He stood there for second with a confused look on his face until he just dropped dead hitting the floor hard.

Envy's hand was shaking with her gun still aimed. "Oh my fucking God," she screamed out nervously and scared at the same time.

"Calm down, baby. You did good," Michael replied as he noticed tears rolling down her face and her whole body shaking from shock and fear.

"I just shot and killed that man," she said with tears in her voice.

"You had to baby. You know it was them or us," Michael replied as he took her in to his arms. They held then heard a noise that broke their embrace and quickly aimed their guns towards it. Mike was getting off the floor. Both Envy and Michael almost forgot that he was there. Mike looked at them both and smiled then the three of them faced the first gunmen Envy shot. He was still alive, but bleeding from the hole in his neck and chest. His eyes were open as he held his neck with both hands to try and stop the blood gushing out. His legs were jerking while he sat on the floor and he knew in his heart it was only a matter of time before he died. His body was getting cold and he felt sleepy. "No, I got to fight it. I must not go to sleep," he said over and over in his head.

Mike walked up to the gunmen and watched him choke on his own blood. Their eyes met as Mike dug in his pocket and pulled out his switchblade and flicked it open. "You wanted to hurt my family?" he yelled and began to swing hard and fast with all his might. The knife went in and out of the gunmen cutting and stabbing him. The gunmen jerked and shook as his body slid more to the floor. His eyes never left Mikes and his last thought was 'I've been killed by the devil' as his body jerked up and down and he died. Mike seen the man was no longer moving, but that still didn't stop his rage. He now had both of his hands locked on his knife and raised it high above his head and was coming all the way down with full force repeatedly. "You tried to hurt my family! Die! Die!" he screamed.

Michael and Envy stood there mesmerized at what they were seeing. "Mike stop! Stop!" both of them yelled, but it was as if he was in another world and couldn't hear them. Michael jumped out the shower followed by Envy. The more he stabbed the more blood splattered on him and everywhere else. Michael grabbed him from behind and lifted him up. "Stop, Mike, calm down! Stop!" Mike continued to swing and wiggle around almost stabbing Michael. Michael had to drop him. "Mike, stop now!" Envy yelled as loud as she could. He turned around and looked at her and Michael with a deranged look in his eyes with the knife in one hand and breathing hard. Then the look vanished as fast as it came.

"I'm sorry Envy. I couldn't help it. What's wrong with me?" he said with tears in his voice and he dropped the knife and began to cry. "You and Michael are mad at me now and you're going to send me away now," he started to cry even harder looking at them both.

Envy didn't know what to make of the

whole situation. She had two dead men on her bathroom floor and a ten year old child that was now covered in blood from stabbing a man to death and now crying.

Michael threw Envy a towel and she wrapped it around her body as he did the same with another towel. He bent down and looked at Mike in the eyes. So much of the boy reminded him of himself, even from the way he just blacked out and lost control. "Don't cry we're not going to send you away. We are your family now," Michael replied as he hugged Mike and he hugged him back.

He picked him up and walked out of the bathroom and his room and down the hall to Mike's room. "Listen, stop crying, Mike. Everything is alright now. You did good. You have to learn how to control your anger and yourself from blacking out."

"But I can't. I don't even know when it's happening. I just don't feel like myself or it feel good. I can't stop," Mike replied with tears in his eyes rolling down his face.

"I understand. I black out the same way. But I recently learned how to have some control over it. You have to think of everyone you have and all the good things in life and all the good you have to do." Mike began to shake his head up and down.

"I'll try."

"Do more than try. Do it every time it happens."

"Do you think Envy is mad at me?"

"No, she's not mad at you. She just not use

to all this. But she will be ok. Now, I need you to wash up and get some clean clothes and put them on. Put the bloody clothes in a black garbage bag and bring them to me. I would ask you for the knife that you always carrying around, but I have a feeling that you won't part with it." As soon as Michael said those words, Mike put his hands behind his back to hide the knife. "I see I got my answer. Ok, you can keep it. I have a thing for a knife too. But clean it up with some bleach really good. I'll be back in a half an hour. I'm going to tend to Envy alright."

"Ok," Mike replied and wiped his tears that was mixed with blood.

Michael went into the bedroom. Envy was fully dressed with her hands buried in the palm of her face sniffing and sobbing. He sat down on the bed next to her and wrapped his arms around her body. "Stop crying, it's ok, it's over now?"

"I know Michael, but it's just too much to handle. I can't believe what just happened. I think I need to go to my sister's house for a while." Envy stated.

"What you're leaving me now over some bullshit?" Michael couldn't help what happened he said feeling hurt with the thought of Envy leaving him.

"Oh baby no I am not leaving you no matter what happens. I just need a break from this house for a while to clear my head. You know me once I go shopping for some shoes that will make me feel a little better. Besides what are we going to do about the bodies and this mess? Well, we sure can't call the cops after Mike done stabbed one of them up so bad if he hadn't done that we could have said they broke in the house. It would've been self defense if only it was a gunshot wound."

"Yea, but Envy the cops will still try to hold us for gun charges and ask where did the guns come from at least no one heard the shot cause we put those silencers on them. So I'm going to dump those bodies somewhere." Michael said while looking her in the eyes.

"You realize that we can't live here anymore? This place will never be safe between Pooky and who ever that man is that's helping him and my father knowing my where about. We will never be able to sleep in here it's not safe anymore. This will continue to happen. I have to worry about your safety and Mikes. One thing that I learned from Black Ice is how to save money and have more than one place to rest my head. That is how that nigga survived. He had many houses and apartments that no one knew about. So, we will always have a place to hide until he was ready to strike again."

"So Michael, what are you saying? You're saying we have to move, but where and how."

"It's easy, baby. I have another place in Roosevelt Long Island that's where we going to be staying for now on," Michael replied.

"What? You mean to tell me you have other houses all this time? I thought we were staying here because we had no other place to go. And be together, but you been here because your waiting on your father?" she screamed. "I can't believe you.

Your ass is crazy."

"I am sorry Envy, but like I said. I'm ready for my father no matter what house we're in or where. I need to know and be ready for when he comes for me. Shit, my mother is a church woman now and she got guns all over her house in places just like mines. There's not a room you walk in that she's not ready because she knows we have to be ready when the devil as she call him comes." Then Michael's mothers words ran though his mind, 'you have to be ready my son and armed. Always stay on point because he is the devil in the flesh.' His mind stopped racing and he looked back at Envy. "Stop yelling, baby, you knew what you was getting into when you became my woman. So, it ride or die baby."

Envy took a deep breath. She knew what he was saying was true she knew. Shit everyone knew the stories of Black Ice. They were told in every hood over and over like he was the boogeyman. Sometime as you get older you have to wonder were the stories real or maybe just stories to keep You in check and afraid of the dark and weird looking men. But people don't believe in the boogeyman or what they said about Black Ice until You saw it with your own eyes. "Ok Michael, I am down with you cause you know that I love you until death do us part." They kissed deeply and passionately. "But, baby, I still need a day away from here and I'm going to my sister's place. That will help me think."

"Well ok love, just call me when you get there and call when you want me to pick you up to go to the other house. Or if you want to follow me there later it's up to you. It does not matter as long as you're happy. Now, you have the other house to decorate," Michael said with a smile. He knew that Envy loved fashion.

Envy laughed out loud and smiled. "Boy, you know my weakness don't you, but first I'm going to buy me some shoes. So shopping here I come. Got to go release some of this stress."

"But, you have over two hundred shoes," Michael stated.

"You know women never have too many shoes. We need shoes for every pocket book, jeans, dress, and lip stick and sometimes the color of our nails and hair." They both started laughing.

Michael stopped laughing and went under the bed and pulled out a hunting knife with a purple handle and a holster that strapped to the leg. "My mother gave you the 3.57 with the holster to strap to your right thigh and I feel you need a knife. You never know when you need it. I know you have three guns already. The twin 40 caliber guns that go around your shoulders and the 3.57 magnum on your right leg, but I want something on your left for me just to feel safe.

"God damn, I feel like I'm going to war," she stated.

"You are. Bullets may run out and you still have a knife to work with. You have to be able to handle yourself for whatever comes your way. Trust me everything I teach you and everything I tell you to carry will come in handy someday. And you'll be more than able to handle yours," Michael stated.

"Ok, I'm only taking it because the handle is my favorite color." Envy replied and strapped the knife to her thigh under her jeans then pulled them up and put on her leather jacket to cover the two guns she was carrying. It was October so it was easy to hide all the weapons under her clothes. Everything she had on matched down to her shoes as always. She thought about the knife on her thigh and her mind flashed back to Mike stabbing that man to death. It kept running though her head like a movie. Black Ice always uses some type of knife or blade on his victims and from what I heard about Michael he chopped up anyone who was beating or abusing women or who were selling drugs around the community center that is why they called him Evil. I don't know how true that is, but he always kept a knife strapped to him. I never seen him black out in front of me and hurt anyone. But I always know he has it and somehow Black Ice passed down his demon ways to Michael and Mike. I don't know how I'm going to tell Michael that Mike is his brother she thought for a moment. Now is not the time or the place and this wasn't it. I'll have to let him know the truth about Mike soon. "Michael, I'm going now," Envy said as she stopped her mind from wandering and grabbed her purse. "I'll call you when I'm ready for you to come and get me to take me to the new house. We need to have a talk about something as well."

"Okay?" Michael replied as he kissed her goodbye. He didn't want her to go, but knew she had to have a life outside of his too.

Envy walked down the hall and she went in Mike's room to check on him. He was fully dressed with the South Pole green shirt and jeans with the sneakers to match that she had got for him. Mike looked up at her as if he wanted to cry. "Are you mad at me, Envy?"

She looked down at him into his eyes that looked so innocent on his handsome face. How could someone look like that and have so much evil in them she thought to herself. "No baby, I'm not mad at you. I was never mad at you just that I'm shocked at all that happened today."

He smiled knowing now that she was not mad at him and the fact that she still loved him. He didn't want to lose her love that made him feel good all over.

"I'm going away for a day or two then I'll be back okay Mike?" Envy told him.

His facial expression changed as soon as the words were spoken. "I thought you said you wasn't mad or upset with me, Ms. Envy? Please, don't go, I need you. You're so nice to me and no one has ever been so nice to me. But you and Michael dress me nice and feed me. You gave me my own room and a bed to sleep in." Mike began to cry. "Please, don't leave! I'll be good. I couldn't help it."

Envy hugged him and kissed his forehead. "No baby, I'm not leaving. I'm just going to see my sister for a day and go shopping. You know how I love to shop. It helps me smile. I'll never leave you. We are family now." Envy stated rocking him and began to cry herself seeing Mike so upset and crying and the pain he was carrying.

He was so young, but seemed so old for his age. Both Mike and Envy held each other until they stopped crying. "Okay, let's stop all this crying." She wiped his face and wiped the tears away from her face with her hands. "I'll come back."

"Okay Ms. Envy," Mike said and smiled she kissed his forehead.

"Later Mike, goodbye," she turned around and said to him.

"Never say goodbye. Goodbye is forever. Say see you later." They both smiled and she walked down the hall.

She unlocked the door and headed out. She wondered how the gunmen got into the house as she got in her white BMW. She started the car and sat there lost in her mind thinking as the car was warming up. They both are so worried about me, but the fact is, that there's two dead men upstairs in the bathroom. Killing and death is so naturally for them. It's like it's almost normal as if it's second nature she said out loud as she headed towards her sister's house.

Mike knocked on Michael's door. He opened it with a black bag in his hand. "Hey, you alright?" Michael asked.

"Yes, I'm okay," Mike replied.

"Good because I'm ready to bounce. You ready? Let's go." Michael said and took the bags and took one last look at the place with the two dead men on the bathroom floor then headed out the door.

He jumped in his Lexus and took off. Michael pulled up in front of his community center in Brownsville. Mike smiled as he looked at the building. He missed playing with the other kids so much. The place felt like home. Mike jumped out of the car and ran to the front door followed by Michael. He grabbed Mike's hand. Remember don't tell anyone what happened this morning."

Mike shook his head yes up and down and ran in the building. Michael did his rounds to see how many women and children were staying there. He was also checking on his staff. He went back downstairs and saw Mike playing football in the gym. "He'll be ok. I got to get this done." Michael said and quickly left the center and began driving back to his house.

Once in the house, he began wrapping up the bodies. He carried the bodies to his car one by one after making sure no one was around or looking out their windows. He began bleaching down everything in the house the bathroom more than anything. He was scrubbing the wall and the floors. He put everything bloody in a bag with Mike's clothes in it. He locked the house door and jumped into his car and took off. He drove straight to the house in Flatbush, parked in the garage, and then pulled the bags with the bodies in them in the house. He dragged them into the basement where he opened a suitcase that had knives and machetes of all different sizes. He picked up the longest one and unwrapped the bodies making sure that the plate covered the floor. He began to chop them up, piece by piece, from their head to their legs and arms. He then carried the body parts upstairs to the second floor to a room far in the back. He never really entered this room something about it he just didn't like. As he unlocked the door, the cold air hit his face. This was different from the rest of the other rooms. This room was turned into a freezer. The other rooms all had the body parts in jars, big and small, but not here. The body parts were hung from hooks from heads to arms and even half of a man's body. Michael knew this room was where Black Ice had put the people he hated the most. Michael hung up the body parts on the hooks and quickly left the room. Then he changed his clothes making sure to wash all of the blood off of himself. He left the house and headed back to the community center.

Mike sat in the cafeteria at a table eating pizza and drinking juice. He was tired of playing with the other kids so he sat alone. The cafeteria was packed with children from all ages and gender. A little girl, that was ten years old, seen Mike by himself and walked over to him with her tray of food in her hand. "May I sit with you?" she asked.

Mike looked up from his tray and when he saw the girl he couldn't help, but to smile. She was dark skinned with her hair all braided up with beads. Her eyes were almond shaped and her smile was as bright as the sun. She had a sweater that looked too big for her and some dirty jeans with some beat up looking sneakers on. "Sure you can sit," Mike replied.

"Okay thanks. My name is Crystal and you are?"

"My name is Mike."

"Oh okay. Hi Mike, it's nice to finally talk

to you," Crystal replied.

"What you mean by that?" Mike asked.

"Well I always see you around here, but you never say anything to me. You play with some of the other kids then always sit alone somewhere and watch what everybody else is doing."

Mike smiled. "So, you're watching me, but yeah I just like to be alone sometimes," he replied while taking another bite of his pizza.

"Me too, Mike. So, maybe we can be alone together as friends." Crystal said with a cheesy smile on her face hoping she made a new friend.

"Okay that sounds good to me. So how old are you, Crystal?"

"I'm ten years old about to be eleven in November."

"Oh okay I'm ten. My birthday is in May. So, who are you here with?" Mike asked.

Crystal stopped eating her pizza and her facial expression changed. She got so sad. "Umm, my mommy. She just came back. Now, she's smoking that funny smelling stuff and is too pretty for that. She used to smoke her cigarettes that didn't smell so bad and when she was done she cooked and we ate a lot." Crystal face lit up when she thought about it then got sad again. "Then she went missing one day so I came here because no one else wanted me, not my aunties or grandmother. I stayed here for three months without telling anyone she was gone because I knew they would take me away like they do to the other kids who don't know where their mommy or daddy is at."

"So, what happened?" Michael asked

knowing now how much he could relate to her life.

"Well, one night she just came back and didn't look or smell the same, but I knew it was her. She found me here and came to visit and check up on me, but kept leaving to go back to find more of that funny smelling stuff to smoke out of a glass pipe. I cried and cried and asked her to stop and she said she would try. She said we had no place to live in the projects. We lost everything, but everyone knew the center would help. They feed you, wash your clothes, and give you a place to sleep upstairs. So, mommy said to stay here and ever since she left and came back she hasn't been acting like she used to. She talks in her sleep, screams, and cries. Every time I talk to a boy she yells and says they will rape me. All boys and men will rape me like they did her."

Mike had a confused look on his face. He understood everything she was talking about until she said rape. "Crystal, don't laugh at me, but what is rape?"

"Well, my mommy said that's when a boy or a man touches your body or your private parts and you yell stop, but they keep doing it. That's rape. When my mommy sleeps, she fights like a lot of men are touching her where they shouldn't in her dreams. Mommy said all boys and men are bad, but I don't believe that. Mr. Michael, who owns this place, isn't bad and he's helping mommy get a place of her own to live. Mike, you're not bad. You wouldn't hurt me right?" Crystal asked looking him in the eyes.

"No, I wouldn't. Michael taught me over

and over to never hurt girls. It's wrong for a man or a boy to do so."

"Okay so that's great. I'm done eating. Let's go play." Crystal said as she got up and looked back to see if Mike was going to come. Mike and Crystal played for the rest of the day. They played cards and tag and video games in the game room. The center staff had them watch a Disney movie with the rest of the kids in the movie room.

Michael was back at the center and loved how it was running. So far they cleaned up ten women for good off crack and helped to get section eight apartments this month alone. The state was helping fund his center through grants, but in the back of his head he knew that he'd never been able to get this started without the money he found so many years ago in the houses that his father left him. "It's funny Black Ice sells crack to women and I clean them up," he said out loud as he looked at the intake paper work in his office. He noticed that there seemed to be more young women coming in pregnant and addicted to crack. It didn't make sense. Most young people don't smoke crack. They mostly get abused women. "Something is going on," Michael thought out loud. Michael put the paper work away and left his office. He made his last run checking on security guards and counselors that would be working the night shift. It was 8pm and time for the cafeteria to serve dinner then a snack, but some of the children were still in the movie room watching another Disney movie. Michael knew that's where he would find Mike.

Some of the counselors were at the movie room door and telling the children to go eat. Outside the room Mike and Crystal were talking about the movie. Michael smiled at seeing this. Out of nowhere a woman came and grabbed Crystal by the arm and turned her around to face her. "Didn't I tell you not to talk to boys or men? They're evil and will hurt you," the woman screamed and squeezed tighter on Crystal's arm.

"Mommy, you're hurting me and Mike is my friend. He wouldn't hurt me."

"Crystal don't you fucking talk back to me. Don't speak to no boys."

Michael had seen enough. He knew Candice well. She was Crystal's mother. He also knew that she was a good person, but she hasn't been the same once she went missing. Every time a man tries to touch her, she would jump out of fear. Michael had sat down and talked to her over and over trying to help her and find out what had happened to her during those few months, but she refused to talk. "That's enough you're overreacting. Crystal didn't do anything wrong."

Candice was about to yell 'mind your fucking business this is my child' until she looked up and seen it was Michael standing next to her. "You're right Michael, but I'm scared and think they're all bad and going to hurt my baby like they hurt me."

"You can't think like that Candice. I'm a good guy. Haven't I been there for you?"

"Yes Michael, you have, but you're the only good guy left."

"Well okay, but you see this little boy. His name is Mike. I'm his legal guardian that means I'm raising him. He's a good boy and going to grow up to be a good man. So, he'll never hurt Crystal."

Candice took a minute to let his words run through her mind. She was twenty six years old; dark skinned, and had a body most women killed for until she got hooked on crack. Her look was starting to come back from not smoking. She found Michael to be a very attractive man even though she was older by a few years. She knew he had wisdom far from his age. 'Damn, if I fix myself up, maybe he'll find me beautiful. He's the only man I trust in this world right now,' Candice thought to herself. "Okay Michael, if you say he's good like you, I'll take your word. It's just hard for me to trust any man after what I've been through and seen."

"Yeah Candice, you really need to tell me all about it one day."

Candice just shook her head from side to side, "I can't."

"Okay, we'll finish this conversation another day. It's time for me and Mike to go. "Mike say bye to your friend."

Mike hugged Crystal. "Bye, see you tomorrow."

"Bye Mike," Crystal replied. She wanted to hug him back, but feared what her mother would do or say.

"Bye Candice," Michael said as he walked out of the building with Mike at his side.

Crystal and Candice watched Mike and

Michael leave. “Come on baby, let’s go eat.” Candice said as she touched her daughter by the hand and headed up the stairs. ‘I can never tell what happened to me to Michael or he’d kill me.’ Candice thought to herself as she remembered all the things Black Ice and his men did to her. The main thing he said to her and the other few women he let free a month ago. ‘If you ever talk or tell anyone about what happened to you, I’ll find you and you will suffer and undergo pain for as long as I want to keep you,’ then he laughed. His laughter echoed through her head as she entered the cafeteria. She looked at some of the women eating. They all made eye contact for a while and remembered the dark secret. They would never tell Michael.

“This isn’t’ the way home.” Mike stated as he noticed they were taking a different route.

“I know Mike, but we’re going to our new home.”

“But why aren’t we going back to our old house? I like it there and liked my room and bed,” Mike replied while getting sad. It was his first time having his own room and own bed in his whole life. He remembered when the social workers would bring him to a new foster home the foster parent would be nice at first and showed him a room and bed and say it was his, but as soon as the social worker left he was forced to sleep on the floor or sometimes the stairs.

Michael looked at Mike’s face from the corner of his eyes. “Mike, listen the new house is better and you still will have your own room and always will because we're family. As soon as Envy is done clearing her head and visiting her sister, she'll go shopping for the house to really make it look nice. We both know how much she loves to shop and make things look pretty." Mike and Michael both smiled because they knew fashion was Envy's life. "So tell me about your new friend, Crystal."

"Well, she's nice to me and funny and likes to be alone sometimes just like me. We talk a lot about everything. I wouldn't even know that she was a girl sometimes because she was so cool."

Michael laughed at seeing Mike smile over his new friend. "Well Mike, some girls are cool, but I'm going to tell you what my mother always told me 'Women are like flowers. Treat them with a gentle touch and never hurt them.' Okay?"

"Okay Michael." Mike's eyes got wide as they pulled up in the driveway of a beautiful two story house. "There's grass. I've never seen grass in front of a house before."

Michael looked at Mike as if he were crazy. Then he remembered that Mike was only used to living in Brooklyn in the projects or buildings. Mike jumped out of the car as soon as it stopped and looked at the house. "Wow!"

"Come in. If you like the outside, you're going to love the inside," Michael stated as he opened the front door. Mike couldn't believe how big it was inside and so nice. He ran from room to room looking at everything until he found a bedroom with his name on it. He opened the door and smiled. The room was all blue and had a big bed and even his own television. “Do you like it? I know I’m not as good as Envy when it comes to decorating, but she will add more to it when she comes.”

“I love it Michael, thank you.” Mike said and hugged him and tears of joy came rolling down his face.

“I packed all of your clothes and things from the old house and brought it here. I even got something for you up under your pillow.”

Mike walked to his bed and looked up under the pillow and pulled out a four inch hunting knife with a holster. “This is for me?” Mike asked while pulling out the shiny, sharp knife out of the holster and looked at it.

“Yeah Mike, it’s for you, but you have to promise not to black out and not to carry it all the time. The switch blade you carry in your pocket everywhere is fine, but this is a little bigger. You’ll have to keep it strapped to your thigh up under your jeans in the holster. Never pull it out, unless you really, really need to and most of all God please don’t tell or show Envy you got that. She’ll kill us both.”

“Okay Michael. I love it and will keep it clean and safe because it’s from you.”

“Remember Mike, when you black out think of the people you love and who loves you and control it. I know I shouldn’t give you that, but I had more than a few knives at your age and shit I got a lot now,” Michael said with a smirk. “I also know you know how to protect yourself, me, and Envy. We never know when that may take place, okay?"

Mike was so zoned out from looking at his new knife. He only heard a few words of what Michael said. "Yeah okay, Michael," he replied.

"Okay, we're going to eat and then get ready for bed. We have another long day tomorrow."

"It feels funny with everyone not being here." Mike said as he put the knife back up under his pillow.

"Yeah I know, but she won't be gone for long."

Envy's stress was finally leaving slowly, but surely. She spent the day shopping with her sister buying shoes that always helped her no matter what the situation was. Envy was now trying on her new pair of shoes inside her sister's Kema apartment. "Ooow girl, those red heels are too fly." Kema said as she watched Envy walking back and forth modeling them off.

"I know right," Envy replied while touching her hair and tossing it backwards like she was a super model causing Kema and her both to laugh. Kema then tried on a pair of black heels that had a gold zipper on the side of them. "Damn, I love these shoes," Kema said while standing up from the couch and looking at them. Kema was just four years older than Envy and even at twenty- three you could tell they were sisters. They had the same smile and caramel complexion and that voluptuous shape with their long, flowing hair that came to their shoulders. Their body type is what you call a thick woman with a whole lot of booty. "Okay Envy, we've been shopping for a day and a half now and you been staying at my apartment and your welcome to stay as long as you want. I'm not saying I don't love shopping shit spend that hard earned money on my ass, but what's really going on girl? There's a reason why you not home with that sexy ass man of yours."

Envy looked at her sister and knew she could read her like a book then sat down on the brown leather couch. "There's so much going on, Kema. First, me and Michael took a little boy from the community center named Mike and I've grown to care and love him. But, here's the fucked up part, the social workers sent me his papers and I found out his real name and that the little boy is really Michael's brother."

"What? Do Michael know?" Kema asked with a shocked look on her face.

"No, I didn't tell him. I just found out the other day and I was about to tell him then some crazy shit came up."

"So, are you going to tell him soon?" Kema asked.

"Yes, I am. I have to. I still have the papers in my purse, but that's not the worse part that I'm about to tell you and I'm only telling you because I can trust you. We all know the stories of Black Ice and the things he did or they say that he do and that Michael is his son. So now we living in the house that Black Ice left him and got to worry about when he will come and get Michael."

"But, Envy you knew all of this before you got with Michael or moved in."

"Yeah Kema, I did, but now he has more

enemies. His cousin, Pooky tried to kill him one night by the center, but Michael handled it. The other day two gunmen broke into our house that worked for Pooky. I shot and killed one and Michael killed the other one."

"So, what's wrong with that Envy? Shit, if someone breaks into my apartment, I'll kill their ass too." Kema said while pulling out a chrome baby 9 mm from her purse. "I know grand mom raised us, but we live on these streets and know we have to protect ourselves as women. I taught you how to use a gun when you were fourteen. So tell me, what's the problem, Envy? You have a good man that helps women and children, you go to school, and he loves you."

"Kema, I know how good my man is. There's just crazy shit going on. I done seen that little boy, Mike, black out and start stabbing the dying gunmen I shot. We had to yell and pull him off the guy to snap him back. Shit, he's only ten years old and that makes me think what if Michael blacks out like that? I won't be able to control him. I heard about his other side. His street name is Evil, but never seen him wild out myself. I know his eyes can get so cold and evil at times, just like that little boy."

"But Envy, you know you can't listen to rumors or the streets. If you did, you know Michael or Evil, as they call him, would never hurt a woman, only men that abuse them," Kema stated.

"I know Michael would never hurt me. I'm just thinking now that there are two boys out there with Black Ice's blood in them and there might be three."

"Envy, you think Black Ice knows that he has another son?"

Envy stopped and thought for a while. "Hell no, if he did, I'm sure he would come for him. He'll be easier to control more than Michael. He always wanted to control him," Envy replied.

"Yeah you're right, so you know you have to be strong and ready. I got your back and what you mean three people with Black Ice's blood in them? There are only two we know about right?"

Envy lowered her head. "Kema, I'm pregnant."

"What girl? That's great!" Kema yelled and hugged her and was smiling from ear to ear. Kema pulled back when she noticed that Envy wasn't smiling. "What's wrong, girl? You're not happy? You don't want the baby?"

"No Kema, it isn't that. I want the baby and I'm happy about it. I just found out when I took the test in your bathroom yesterday because I haven't been feeling so good. I'm sad because what if my baby has Black Ice's rage like Michael or Mike, and even worse, what if Black Ice comes for my baby?"

"That would never happen, ever. Michael would never let that happen and you're a fighter. You wouldn't let that shit happen and I sure as hell won't let that go down."

"Yeah, I know you right girl, that's why I love you. You always clear my head."

"So, when you going to tell Michael about the baby and Mike being his brother?"

Envy looked at her sister in the eyes, "Soon,

real soon."

Chapter 12

"Your mine Roxy, don't you forever forget that!" Black Ice yelled with each pump he made inside Tiffany making sure to give her all that long nine inch dick with hard deep strokes. Tiffany's hands were chained to the wall by her wrist above her head with her back pressed against the wall and legs spread wide open with Black Ice between them pumping fast and hard, then real slow. "Your mine and always will be Roxy!" Black Ice yelled as he pumped even harder.

"Yes, I'm yours. I'm yours," Tiffany screamed back. She could tell by the look in his eyes that she better say what she had to in order to keep him calm. 'Damn, why his dick got to feel so fucking good,' she thought to herself as she came and looked at the sweat dripping down his muscular body onto his six pack stomach and ripped arms with muscles popping out from everywhere. Her pussy couldn't help, but to get wetter. Black Ice pumped as fast as he could go and nutted all inside Tiffany.

"Damn, that's my bitch." He pulled out of her and pulled up his jeans, threw his shirt over his shoulders, and let it hang there. "If you keep being good, I might take your ass out this fucking room with these bitches and my pet hyenas chained to the other side of these rooms."

Tiffany turned her head to see Star hanging right there next to her and Yasmin chained to the wall as well. Tiffany and Star's eyes met and she could see the sadness in them. "I kind of like it in this room," Tiffany said out loud.

Black Ice stopped from walking out of the room and stood there with his back turned. He turned around and pulled out a six inch knife that was curved at the tip. He walked over to Tiffany looking in her eyes. Her whole body began to shake. She knew there was nothing in his crazy mind that he wouldn't do to try and harm her or anyone else. It was as if he fed off of the pain of others. Black Ice raised the knife to her face. "You like it here, Tiffany, in this fucking room and have the nerve to talk back? I think I know why and I will cut the problem at the source." Black Ice moved from Tiffany and walked over to Star. He grabbed her face. "No, please no," Star screamed and began to cry.

"Don't hurt her. Please, don't hurt her. I'll be good."

Black Ice looked at Tiffany then smiled. In one swift move, he swung slicing Star's cheek leaving a wide cut at first you could see the meat and then the blood started to pour out of it. Star screamed out in agonizing pain. He then cut her next cheek. Star cried and screamed. "Please, stop no…no more!"

At the scent of blood, the four hyenas chained up started to get excited and started pulling away from the chains to get away, free to attack.

"Please, I'll be good I swear. I didn't mean what I said!" Tiffany yelled while crying.

"Now, you listen bitch and you listen good," Black Ice said while looking at Tiffany. "You not in this fucking room to enjoy yourself. The only reason your little friend here is alive is because of you as soon as you get that through your head the better. I'll kill her if you try to run again and if you talk back. I'll cut your ass so badly you would wish you were dead. Then I will fuck, Star, here and then cut off her arms then feet and feed her to my hyenas, very slowly. So, she and you both can watch them enjoy their meal. Are we fucking clear?"

"Yes! Yes!" Tiffany screamed and shook her head up and down.

"Ha Ha Ha!" Black Ice laughed. His laughter sent chills through Tiffany, Star, and Yasmin's body even the hyenas stopped laughing and sat down out of fear. As he walked out of the room and the steel door shut behind him, outside the door was one of his henchmen, Tiwan. "How's the drug selling going? Did we make the quota this month?"

"Yes boss. We did better than last month. We made over 300,000 dollars. It's getting easier with all the drug dealers buying all the weight of crack from us. The increase of all the women that we've made crack heads. They go back on the street and sell their bodies or do anything to buy crack even turning their men into crack heads by telling them they would love it if they just tried it," Tiwan replied.

This only made Black Ice smirk his devilish grin. "Yes, just as I planned. I think we soon need to do this in other boroughs and states. Tiwan, I made you in charge of all the other men because of your actions of killing that fool who had no idea and

I think you know better than to cross me right?" Black Ice said as he looked at him from the corner of his eyes.

"No boss. I'm not foolish enough to cross you and will kill anyone thinking of it." Tiwan said meaning every word.

"Good, keep it that way and you'll live long and be rich." Black Ice replied as his mind began to think of Michael. "My boy, you should be ready for me by now. I've let you grow and watched you and know the killer you've become. Soon it will be time to see if you have more of my blood in you or your mother's," he said out loud.

Tiffany and Star both felt as if they both couldn't stop crying. "Don't cry, Star, I swear I'll find a way for us to get out of here. I swear," Tiffany said as she let the last tear roll down her face. "I hate that motherfucker and will get him."

"Tiff we're never going to get out of here. He'll never let us go. He'll feed us to them dogs first. He has something for you and in his sick mind, its love." Star explained while still crying.

Yasmin couldn't help but cry too as she looked and listened to her two friends. "I'm sorry, Tiff and Star. I know we will be alright and we'll get out one day," Yasmin stated.

"Won't you shut the fuck up bitch? I blame your ass for us being in this room. Now, we might have gotten away if we found the door to the parking lot, but you had to sell your own friends the fuck out for an eight ball of crack and the dream of him setting you free. You're no fucking better than him or his men. Two young women died because of you. We are in this room because of you," Tiffany yelled.

"But, I'm sorry, I couldn't help it. That crack was calling me and I wanted to be free. I wasn't thinking straight." Yasmin replied while crying and thinking of her actions.

"What the fuck you mean, you couldn't help it, Yasmin? We've been friends our whole life. We constantly talk to women every day. We talk them through a drug problem and you couldn't help yourself, bitch? I think your true side came out at the end. You only care about yourself, but I swear you are going to fucking get yours." Yasmin held her head down in shame. "Yeah I hope you fucking die or he feed you to them damn dogs, Yasmin."

"Why would you hurt me? I would never hurt you. I love you," Star yelled.

"Don't waste your energy on her, Star. She could care less and she's just waiting for the next time they come in here with some crack for her to smoke. That's the only thing she seems to love now."

"Yeah, you're right, but even as a crack head these monsters made me. I know who my true friends are and where my loyalty belongs," Star replied.

Chapter 13

Envy couldn't believe how beautiful the house was in Long Island and wished they moved there first instead of the town house in Brooklyn. She loved Brooklyn and was a Brooklyn woman all the way, but there was something about Long Island she was starting to love. She spent the day shopping with Michael and Mike buying things for the house. Roosevelt Mall was becoming one of her favorite shopping spots now. "I love this, Michael, decorating is my favorite thing to do next to making myself and people pretty."

"I know, Envy, that's why I let you do it."

"No Michael, you let me do it because I'm great at it," Envy said laughing. "Come on Mike, we have to hurry up and get to the car so we can meet the delivery trucks at home for our new stuff."

"Yes, Miss Envy," Mike replied while walking as fast as his little legs could while carrying three shopping bags in each hand.

"Envy, leave him alone," Michael said laughing while loading bags into the truck and Envy doing the same. Mike had stuffed his bags in the car. "Did you have fun today, Mike?"

"Yes, Miss Envy, I did and thank you for buying the outfits for me and most of all the outfits for my friend, Crystal. Now, she is going to love it with the sneakers."

"It was no problem, Mike, and you can stop calling me Miss Envy baby, just call me Envy, okay?"

"Okay," Mike replied. Michael smiled as

they drove home. He loved the way they interacted with each other. “It’s good to have you back. I was starting to worry that all that happened scared you and besides me and Mike was making a mess of the new house.”

“Oh, don’t blame it on Mike. Michael I know how messy you are at times. The both of you better keep your butts out my living room with the new white living room set coming in. I’ll beat the both of you,” Mike and Michael smiled, but knew Envy meant serious business. As soon as they pulled up to the house, delivery trucks pulled up right behind them and Envy hopped out of the passenger end and started giving orders telling the men what to do and where to put the new couch set and her master bedroom set even a new bed set for Mike’s room.

“Damn, I guess you didn’t like anything I left in the house because you just changed it all,” Michael said as he watched the old things go out and new things come in. He was impressed by Envy’s good taste in fashion. The house became homier with the white living room set, the brown bedroom set for their room, and more. “I guess the saying is true it takes a man to buy a house, but a woman to make it a home.” It took five hours for Envy to get it the way she wanted.

“Okay, now it looks like someone loves the two of you.”

“Someone does love us. You Envy,” Michael replied.

Mike looked at them both and hugged and kissed them. “Umm, you two love me? No one ever said they loved me before." He said then looked down at his feet as if he were scared of what they might say.

"Yes baby, we love you very much. Now, come give us a hug sweetie." Mike lifted his head up and smiled and ran into Envy and Michael's open arms.

"I love you, Mike," Michael said, "We both do."

"I love you too, Michael and Envy." Mike replied as a tear rolled down his face and he hugged them even tighter not wanting to let go for the first time in his life he felt love. He wasn't being beaten or mistreated or someone calling him a child of a crack head that was supposed to take care of him. Envy wanted to cry as she wondered how a child could be mistreated so bad his whole life the same thing that Michael had been through. She felt the only thing different Michael had his mother. Then her mind raced. 'Oh shit, I almost forgot they're brothers. I have to tell them,' Envy thought to herself. "Okay, I guess then I think we should go out tonight and celebrate because of how nice our new home looks," Envy said as she broke their embrace.

"Oh that sounds good to me, baby, and it will give me and Mike a chance to wear one of the outfits you picked out for us."

"Okay, so then it's a date with my two favorite guys. I'll start getting ready and you boys do the same."

Two hours later, Envy, Michael, and Mike were fully dressed and since it was in the middle of

November, they all had on matching gray leather jackets even though under Envy and Michael's jacket their guns were on their shoulder holsters. After living with Michael, Envy knew what it meant to stay on point. So she made it her business to never go anywhere without the guns Rachel gave her and the knife Michael gave her strapped to the holster on her thigh under her jeans. "All my boys look so handsome."

"Thank you, Envy," Mike said.

"These shoes just don't match the gray is too different and my outfit is lighter. Michael, do you think we can step at the old house to grab my other pair of gray Gucci shoes?"

"Damn Envy, out of the hundreds of pairs of shoes you got here and the new ones you brought today, you still can't find a pair to match?" Michael replied.

"No I can't and you know how I am about my shoes. I don't know why you left five pairs behind when you packed and moved my stuff, baby," Envy said while poking her lip out. "Please baby, we'll be in and out then we'll leave. I promise and then we'll never have to go back to that house again."

Michael could see that she wasn't going to be happy until she got her shoes. "Damn spoiled butt, come on. We can stop." Michael said as he headed for the front door followed by Envy who was smiling from ear to ear with Mike holding her hand. They jumped in the car and headed to the belt parkway towards Brooklyn.

A half an hour later they pulled up in front

of their brown stone house. Envy stepped out of the car with the house keys in her hand. "Hold up, baby, I think we all should go in with you," Michael said as he stepped out of the car followed by Mike.

"Yeah, you right." Envy said as she got up the steps to the front door and used the keys to unlock and they then stepped inside. Michael closed the door and pulled his gun out of his holster at the same time as Envy. They walked up their stairs slowly with their guns. Leading the way, Michael opened the bedroom door and looked around. "Grab your shoes and let's get the fuck out of here. I got a bad feeling we shouldn't be here."

"Oh baby," Envy said as she quickly went in the closet and grabbed the Gucci shoe box and the other boxes. Michael just looked at her and shook his head. "What, I'm not leaving my shoes," Envy said as she raised her eyebrow and then followed him and Mike to the front door. Then they put their guns back in their holsters before walking outside and got in the car.

"You happy now, baby?" Michael asked as he pulled off.

"Yes baby, I am," Envy replied while pulling the Gucci shoes out of the box and took off the shoes she had on and put the gray Gucci's on.

"See, I told you Pooky if we wait here they'd come back," Caesar said as he started up the black truck.

"I think we should've of attacked them when they was in the house or when they came out. We have more than enough men with us," Pooky stated as he turned his head around from the passenger seat to look at the four gunmen sitting in the back and could see the next truck parked two cars down with five of their gunmen in it.

"Now, we don't know what they might have had in that house. It could have been a death trap for us and them men. We still haven't heard from the two men. I told your ass not to send them and I know they're dead somewhere," Caesar replied.

"I couldn't wait. I had to see if we could catch him off guard. The motherfucker cut off half my dick and that little ass punk kid cut off a piece of my ear," Pooky yelled back.

"You fool, do you really believe just two men could kill him? He's Black Ice's son. He didn't get the name Evil for nothing. I told your ass to wait till you heal up then make a plan to trap and kill him, but no your ass had to send two of our best men. I want revenge on them, too. Black Ice killed my son and showed me a death I never seen, but I'm still here. We're going to kill his son and him and slowly take over his business."

"Yeah, you're right, Caesar," Pooky said out loud as he thought on how they were always able to find men to work for them with the promise of taking over the Brooklyn drug trade and taking down the most feared and unseen drug lord in Brooklyn.

"We're going to follow them to see where they go," Caesar said as he drove four cars behind Michael's Lexus with the next truck behind him.

Michael drove four minutes on the Belt Parkway and jumped on the Sunrise Highway until they reached Green Acres Mall and pulled into the parking lot of a restaurant called Bronx BBQ. The parking lot was full of people heading inside to the restaurant and some were outside talking to women standing by their car. As Michael, Envy, and Mike made their way to the entrance of the restaurant, everyone couldn't help but look at them matching down to their shoes like movie stars.

"Damn, Michael look at the line to wait for a table. Is it always like this?" Envy asked as she was barely able to get to the door with Mike holding her hand. "How long we have to wait?"

"Envy, don't worry about that," Michael squeezed through all of the people in line and the people waiting on their table until he seen the manager. "Hey, Tony, how are you?"

"Oh shit, Michael, why didn't you call me and let me know you were coming?" Tony replied.

"Well, it was kind of last minute. You think you can hook me up with a table?"

"For you, Michael, anything come follow me," Michael looked back and waved at Envy to move through the crowd of people with Mike. All the people in line waiting for a table began to ball up their faces in anger. Michael, Envy, and Mike were seated at a table next to the stage.

"Michael, why is there a stage in here, baby?"

"Oh Friday's they have comedy night and on the weekends it's Karaoke."

"What's Karaoke?" Mike asked.

"Well thank God we're here on a Friday because you won't find out. It's where people go up on stage and try to sing a song and I do mean try."

Their waiter came and they placed their order. All three of them ordered snow crab legs with grill shrimp and steak. "Michael, how did you get a table so fast?"

"Well baby, the manager Tony, is a friend of mine. A few months ago, his sister that was only sixteen came to my center. She was hooked on crack pretty bad and stayed at the center for four months and got clean. I always asked how she got hooked on it, but she never told. She just always shook with fear at the question. Once she was clean, Tony and his mom were more than happy and took her home. They haven't found out where she had been missing for almost eight months. She still comes by the center once a month to talk to the counselor and me."

The waiter came and gave them their food. "Come on Mike, hold my hand," Envy said as she took Michael's. "God, thank you for this meal and keep us safe in Jesus name, we pray, amen."

Mike looked up after the prayer and seen Michael breaking his snow crab leg and dipped it in butter and Envy was doing the same. He didn't know if he should eat or not or what to do. It was his first time out and being in a restaurant. "Mike, go ahead and eat. It's just like being at home or at the center the only thing that's changed is us being out as a family."

"Okay," Mike replied and began to bust down his food as the comedians came on stage and told jokes over and over while all enjoyed their meal.

Caesar and Pooky sat in the truck and parked next to them was another truck with five gunmen in it. Pooky watched all the couples running in and out. "Damn, there are some fine women here," Pooky said while looking through the truck's window lusting.

Caesar looked at him and shook his head. "Fool, did you forget that you have no fucking dick? What are you going to do with those women? Use your damn fingers and tongue," Caesar yelled.

Pooky sat back in his seat as he felt embarrassed for a while he did forget that Evil had chopped off half of his dick and now he could never be with a woman again and had a plastic bag strapped to his waist with a tube that traveled to what's left of his dick and was used to help him pee. "I'm going to kill that motherfucker as soon as he comes out of that restaurant."

"No, Pooky, don't overreact. We will wait and continue to follow him to wherever he's living now and just before he goes in his house or apartment, we will attack," Caesar replied.

Pooky shook his head up and down, but his body was full of anger. 'You took my pride when we was just kids and as a man you took my dick. I'll kill you evil. I'll kill you,' Pooky thought to himself.

"You enjoy the food, Mike?" Michael asked as he looked at Mike lean back in his seat rubbing his little stuffed stomach.

"Yes I did, but I think I ate too much," Mike replied. Envy and Michael both laughed because they knew the feeling.

"Michael, I have to tell you something," Envy said while looking at him pay and tip the waiter.

"Okay baby, tell me when we leave here and get in the car. It's too noisy in here."

"Okay baby," Envy replied as she got up and took Mike's hand and headed to the exit of the restaurant with Michael following.

Michael stopped to shake Tony's hands. "I want to thank you again and here's a little something," Michael said as he let go of Tony's hand and left a twenty dollar bill in it.

"Thanks Michael, and no problem and my sister will be up there for a visit next week."

"Okay bye, Tony," Michael said as he followed Envy and Mike out of the door. The cool air hit his face. Envy and Mike both were smiling as Michael held Mike's left hand and Envy's right. The parking lot was still filled with couples coming and going in the restaurant and men talking to women.

Pooky could see Michael clear as he was walking to his car. Pooky moved around in his seat as anger rose in his body. "We should get that fucker here and now," Pooky yelled.

"No Pooky, there's a lot of people around. We got him just as he's about to go into his home. He won't see it coming," Caesar replied as he looked at Pooky's face ball up and getting madder and madder.

"Fuck you, I'm killing him now."

"I said no," Caesar yelled as he tried to grab

Pooky's arm to stop him from jumping out of the truck with a tech nine millimeter in his hand. "Shit," Caesar yelled. "You get with him. It's going down now," Caesar told the four men in the back seat and they hopped out all with chrome tech nine millimeter guns. The five men in the next truck seen Pooky and the other men and hopped out and headed towards their target and they knew it was on. They hopped out of the truck four of them were armed with Mossberg pump shotguns and the last one had Koch 9mm pistols.

A group of women were talking to some guys standing by a Mercedes Benz. "I love your car. You going to let me drive it?" one of the women asked while licking her lips and flirting.

"Sure, if you let me ride you, sexy," the guy replied.

"Well, all of my friends are down for that and hooking up with you boys," the woman replied then turned her head to see Pooky bend low running towards them with a gun in his hand followed by nine other men that were all dressed in black leather jackets with guns. "AAHHH," she screamed as loud as she could. Her friends turned their heads to see what had her so scared and when they did they screamed as well.

Michael looked up as he just got to his car and looked to see why the women were screaming. "Oh shit, Envy, Mike get down it's a hit," Michael yelled as he seen Pooky and the other men run towards him.

Michael pulled both of his arms and put them up under his shoulders and pulled out the two chrome 50 caliber desert eagles with extended clips that his mother gave him.

"Fuck," Pooky yelled as he realized that Michael had seen him coming. He raised his gun and squeezed the trigger. A burst of automatic fire spit out bullets tore and ripped through the screaming women that were standing next to the Mercedes that was next to Michael's Lexus. Their bodies jerked and shook as they screamed in pain and hit the ground and died. Michael dove to the ground hitting the ground with his body half way out from behind the car. He aimed and squeezed the trigger. Boom, boom, boom! The bullets from the 50 caliber desert eagle rang out and went through the parked cars and hit two gunmen. One bullet blew half a gunmen's face off and the other hit the gunmen in the chest sending him flying backwards. "What the fuck! What kind of guns does Evil got," Pooky yelled as he looked at the face of one of his gunmen. At the sound of Michael shooting back, the other seven gunmen began to spread out and looked for cover. People were running everywhere trying to get away as the gunmen fired. Two men got shot in their back as they tried to run to the restaurant. "Fuck you Evil, I will kill you tonight no matter what," Pooky yelled as he continued to send burst of automatic fire in Michael's direction. Michael turned real fast to see where Envy and Mike was. They were now two cars down behind him hiding. Michael smiled knowing they were safe. He got up from the ground and crept around to another car making sure to stay low. As he got to the Mercedes Benz, he could see people's bodies shot up and lay dead. He felt someone grab his leg and aimed his gun down. It was a woman who had been shot up with bullets that ripped through her chest and legs. "Help me, help me," she said as she spit up blood.

"I will just lay there and don't move," Michael said. He then noticed two gunmen running towards him that got tired of shooting and not hitting him with bullets from their Tech 9 mm ripping through the cars. Car alarms were going off. Michael jumped up while running and fired both guns simultaneously. The 50 caliber bullets hit one of the gunmen's legs ripping it off. The next gunmen turn his head to see his friend's legs flew off and him falling face first. As he looked down at his friend, a bullet tore through his neck. "AAHHH," he screamed as a large chunk of his neck went flying off leaving his head hanging off to the side and blood gushing up in the air then his body hit the floor.

"Fuck! Fuck! We got to kill this asshole," Pooky yelled while still ducking behind a car and firing. "It's only one of him and six of us, surround his ass," Pooky yelled.

Michael knew he fucked up. He ran to the wrong side of the parking lot. There was a wall blocking his way and he could only go forward or backwards, but soon couldn't do that as Pooky and his men started to surround him.

Envy peeked from behind the car her and Mike was hiding behind and knew it was time for her to make her move or Michael would die. "Listen Mike, you stay here. I got to help Michael,"

"But I want to help too," Mike replied.

"You are by being safe," Envy replied while crossing her arms and dissing up under her jacket and pulled her twin chrome forty caliber handguns that Michael mother had given her. She swiftly crept behind a car then another one.

"Yeah, we got him surrounded. Yeah, we got you now pussy," Pooky yelled at him and his men continued to fire at the car Michael was hiding behind. The gun pumped his shotgun then fired. He did over and over, not giving Michael a chance to return fire. He smiled as he knew he had him and it was just a matter of time before one of his bullets would hit its target. He stopped smiling as he felt melt press to the back of his head.

"You should have never messed with my man asshole," she yelled as she squeezed the trigger. The bullets crashed into the back of his head and came out of his forehead. His body hit the ground and shook for a while and then stopped.

"Oh shit, we got another shooter. It's his girl," one of the gunmen yelled out and aimed at Envy. Before he could squeeze the trigger, Envy screamed and squeezed the triggers to her twin 40 caliber hand guns simultaneously ten times sending bullets through the gunmen's chest and face. He dropped his gun as his body jerked and shook as the bullets tore and ripped through his body. A chunk of flesh went flying everywhere before he fell onto his knees and died with his eyes opened.

"Fuck! Fuck! No," Pooky grew furious as he realized he only had three men left. "Kill that bitch too," he screamed and aimed at Envy and fired. Envy jumped out the way just as the bullet came flying towards her. There were a couple hiding in the back seat of their car. The bullets ripped through the back door killing them as they held each other.

Michael's face balled up in anger as he seen the gunmen now aiming in Envy's direction. "Leave her alone," he screamed as he fired. Four bullets went through the back window of a car and blew of one of the gunmen's arm then him in the back instantly severing his spinal cord. He looked at his arm on the ground and fell over dead. Pooky didn't know what to do. So, he kept firing wildly. A police siren could be heard as the police car pulled up behind Pooky and his two gunmen. The two cops hopped out of the car with their guns drawn and using their car door as cover. "Okay, freeze drop the fucking gun and turn around slowly," Michael quickly moved low, but fast to the car where Envy was ducking.

"You okay, baby," Michael asked.

"I'm fine, but running out of the bullets," Envy replied.

"Yeah, me too, boo, but you're doing good and the cops are here now, but just stay low until they grab them. That's the only way we know this shit is really over. Where's Mike?"

"He's okay, Michael. He's under a car safe way over there," Envy stated.

People were still screaming and crying. Some were in the restaurant on the floor and some were in their cars hiding and others on the ground of the parking lot dead or bleeding to death.

"I said to drop the fucking guns and slowly turn around," one of the cops yelled.

Pooky looked at his two gunmen letting them know what to do. All three of them turned around as fast as they could, aimed, and fired. Their bullets hit one gunman in his head and the next one in his stomach and chest, but he was still firing. Pooky sent automatic fire from the Tech 9 mm that ripped through the cop's face and car crashing into the windshield and door. The cops slumped over onto the open door they were using as cover and were dead right away, but that didn't stop Pooky from firing making their bodies jerk until he heard a clicking sound letting him know he was out of bullets. He pulled a clip out his jacket pocket and removed the old one and replaced it with the new one and cocked his gun.

Michael looked at Envy as they peeped from the corner of the car they were hiding behind and seen all that happened. "Now Envy," he yelled as they both stood up and aimed and fired. Bullets tore into the back of Pooky's last gunmen who was already losing blood from the gunshot wounds the cop gave him. He dropped dead to the ground. A bullet slumped into Pooky's shoulder and he hit the ground yelling.

"Shit, I'm out of bullets in one of my guns," Envy yelled.

"Me too baby," Michael replied as he put one of his guns back into his shoulder holster and Envy did the same. They checked their clips to see they both had only four bullets left a piece.

Pooky stood up and fired while screaming.

Michael grabbed Envy and pulled her down to the floor then fired. A bullet crashed into his right butt cheek leaving a large hole. Pooky dropped to the ground in pain as the smell of burning flesh and blood mixed with urine hit his nose. "I hate you Evil. I fucking hate you," Pooky yelled and continued to fire sending bullets everywhere. He was now on his knees.

"Damn, I can't get a good shot. He's firing too crazy," Michael yelled.

"Yeah, me neither."

Mike stood low and crawled up under all the cars until he was now close enough. He was so small he knew Pooky couldn't see him. He unbuttoned his jeans and pulled out the five inch hunting knife from the strap holster that Michael had given him. He buttoned back his jeans then pulled out the switch blade from his jeans. Mike crawled up under the car. Pooky stopped screaming and swung the gun wildly while firing as he couldn't believe what he was seeing. "That's the little fucker that took a piece of my ear," he said to himself as he noticed Mike ten feet in front of him standing next to a car. Then he noticed that he was holding the knife by the blade. "I remember you. You're dead, you little fucker!"

Before he could get the words out of his mouth, all he seen was the five inch knife flying towards him and that was the last thing his right eye seen as it flew right into it. "AAHHH," Pooky yelled and dropped his gun as he grabbed the knife and pulled it out of his eye socket. He threw down the knife and held his head to his right eye that was now gone. "AAHHH, I'm going to kill you and Evil," Pooky screamed while crying with the one good eye he had left. He grabbed his gun and looked up and when he did the switch blade went flying into his left eye. "AAHHH," Pooky screamed and squeezed the trigger to the Tech 9 mm. Mike moved before he could get hit. "I can't see. I can't see. Caesar, help me! Caesar, help me please," said Pooky while firing wild and crazy.

Michael stood up and fired sending a bullet blowing a hole through Pooky's chest. He fell backwards and was now firing his gun up in the air until he heard a clicking sound. Michael and Envy stood over him and Pooky couldn't see. "I hate you Evil and that little fucker, but don't kill me. We're family."

"Fuck you! You just tried to kill my family. We're not family," Michael said with a smirk on his face then looked at Envy. They aimed their guns to Pooky's head and squeezed the triggers bullets ripped through Pooky's skull until it ripped open and his brain and blood oozed out. Michael picked up Mike's hunting knife and pulled the switch blade out of what was left of Pooky's left eye. "Come, we got to go now," Michael yelled while picking Mike up in his arms and putting him in the back seat and Envy grabbed her purse she left on the ground next to the car. She never noticed the yellow envelope that fell out as she hopped in the car and they took off.

Caesar sat in the truck the whole time watching everything that went on. He heard Pooky call out his name for help, but he refused to move.

He stepped out of the truck and looked around at all his dead men and other people that got caught in the cross fire. He walked pass Pooky's body and his stomach turned at what he'd seen. "I told you boy not to attack them here. There was too many people and places they could hide, shit!" Caesar turned his head as he heard police sirens getting closer. He was about to get back in the truck and leave until something caught his eye. He walked over to where Michael's car was parked and picked up the yellow envelope. As he looked up, he could see people in the restaurant peeping their heads through the window and out of the door and knew it was time for him to go. He jumped in the truck and pulled off just as the cops pulled up he drove passed them.

Once on the highway to Brooklyn he slowed down. Then he pulled over in East New York, Brooklyn. He opened the envelope and began to read and couldn't believe his eyes. "Roxy's baby is alive. Shit, that little boy is her and Black Ice's? I wonder if he knows he's alive. It don't matter I now have two sons of his to kill. Ha! Ha! Ha! Ha," Caesar laughed as he pulled off.

Michael cleaned off Mike's knives then walked into his room. Mike was in his bed up under the covers, but he couldn't sleep until he had his switch blade up under his pillow to feel safe. He got used to it after having all of his foster parents beat him while he was asleep or just beat him for no reason. His knife was his only friend until now. "Here Mike, you did good, but I need you to be safer. Me and Envy will go crazy if something happens to you," Michael said as he handed Mike his knife.

"I'm sorry. I just wanted to help and you're supposed to help family, right?"

"Yeah, that's right, but me and Envy's job is to take care of you, not the other way around."

"Yeah, he's right," Envy said as she entered the room. "Next time, stay where I tell you baby, okay?"

"Okay Envy and Michael, but why they keep trying to hurt us?" Mike asked.

"I don't know, but some people are bad like that and just want to hurt us. But the thing we did, you know we must never tell anyone like that thing that happened to that mean foster mother that used to beat you. People wouldn't understand that we got to protect ourselves, okay?"

"Yeah, I understand, Michael. I'll never tell. This is my family. I love you and Envy."

"We love you too. baby," Envy said as she kissed him on the forehead.

"Goodnight," Michael said as he kissed him on the head as well.

Michael and Envy went to their bedroom. Envy pulled out some weed and a backwoods and rolled up a blunt. Michael wanted to say something. He hated when she smoked, but she only did it when she was stressed with too much on her mind. He hated any and all kinds of drugs because of what it did to his family. "Envy, are you okay, baby?"

"No Michael, that shit was fucking crazy tonight. We was out to just have a good time as a family and we have an army of men trying to kill us."

"I know baby, but with Pooky dead this shit should be over," Michael replied.

"Michael, just because Pooky is dead don't mean shit. This will keep happening. What about the older men with long dreads that saved Pooky the last time he attacked you at the center and I think he called out his name tonight, Caesar, that's who he was asking to help him and we still have worry about your father."

Michael sat on the bed next to Envy and knew she was right. This wouldn't be the last time they will be attacked and knew that Black Ice was out there somewhere just waiting to come get him. 'Caesar, I know that name from somewhere when I was a child,' Michael thought to himself as he turned on the television and changed to the news.

"There has been a blood bath at Green Acres Mall at a restaurant parking lot with more than thirty people shot and killed when nine men fully armed came firing their weapons. Police officer's have been killed and five others injured. No one knows why the men came shooting or if this was just a robbery gone wrong. We know there were other shooters that helped save the people here, but none of the witnesses are talking at all about what they have seen."

Michael turned off the television. "We have to go visit my mother for new guns and get rid of the ones we used tonight. I know none of these people are going to talk and anyone who seen us died from those crazy gunmen," Michael stated.

"This shit is crazy," Envy said as she

continued to smoke. "How did they find us?"

Michael looked at Envy in the eyes as if she really had the nerve to ask that with just one look Envy knew. "It was because of me, right, because we went back to the brown house for my shoes. They were watching the house. I know that now," Envy said as she felt bad for her actions. "Michael, this shit is crazy. I love you, but I don't know how I'm going to deal with this shit. We got niggas trying to kill us and we have a ten year old that's throwing fucking knives and stabbing people and sleeping with them just to feel safe. I know you got that knife for him. This shit isn't normal, Michael. I'm pregnant and my child is going to grow up to be like you and Mike because we're always going to have to teach our children how to kill or protect themselves," Envy said crying.

Mike had to sneak out of his room and had his ear to Michael and Envy's door. After feeling he heard too much, he crept back to his room. 'So, Envy's pregnant that means she'll be having a baby and will Michael and her still love me?' Mike said out loud to himself as he fell asleep.

"Baby, no matter what we'll be safe. I don't want my life like this, Envy. Did you say you're pregnant, Envy?"

"Yes Michael, I'm pregnant. It was the good news I wanted to tell you at the restaurant tonight."

Michael smiled from ear to ear. "Yeah, we're having a baby," he then hugged and kissed her on the lips. "I'm so happy."

"I'm happy too, Michael, but are we going

to be able to keep Mike and our baby safe?"

"I promise. I'll keep us safe," Michael replied.

"I know, baby. I believe you. It's just so much is happening and I'm not at all used to this. Michael, I have to show you something else too and I really don't know how you're going to take it," Envy said as she got off the bed and walked to her purse to dig through it.

"What you looking for, baby?" Michael asked.

"A yellow envelope, with Mike's paper work in it. I had it in my purse. I must've dropped it during the gun fight."

"Envy, what's so important about Mike's paper work?"

"It's what I wanted to tell you. I didn't know how to tell you and was just going to show you. Every time I was about to, something came up, but I'm tired of carrying this and you not knowing, baby."

"Envy, what is it? What have you not been telling me," Michael asked.

Envy took a deep breath then looked Michael in the eyes. "You know how Mike said his mother died from overdose of crack and he was born just in time before she died and he didn't know who his father was and that he was raised in foster care? Well, it's not all true."

Michael looked at Envy with a lost look on his face not really knowing where she was going with all of this. "Envy, you're not making any sense or I'm just not understanding you," Michael stated.

"Baby, Mike's mother didn't die from overdose from crack. She was shot in the head and died after giving birth to Mike. The killer was your father, Black Ice. The woman's name was Roxy Jazzer. Also, Mike's father is Black Ice. There was a DNA test done when he was born that Detective Roy, Sr. authorized because they already had Black Ice's DNA on file from one of his cigarette buds he left at a crime scene. Mike's real name is Michael Jazzer. It was the last words his mother said.

Michael's jaw dropped as he stood there stuck on stupid. His mind raced. 'Roxy, that name my mother used to say a lot for one of the reasons my father first started acting up and began smoking. Mike is my fucking little brother. In my heart, I knew he was connected to me in some kind of way. His eyes are just like mine. He even looks like me and has my ways, but are they really my ways or our father's ways,' Michael thought to himself. "Envy, how the hell could you keep this from me? This isn't some shit you just hold back," Michael yelled.

"Stop yelling, Michael, you're going to wake up Mike and we don't need that. I've been trying to tell you baby. We kept getting attacked left and right from the shower to the parking lot. Don't be mad at me, Michael."

Michael stood up and walked back and forth around the room holding his head. "Shit! Shit! How am I going to tell Mike and I wonder if my father knows about him?"

"Baby, we will tell Mike together when the

time is right and I don't think your father knows about him," Envy stated.

"You're right, baby, I'm sorry for yelling, but I would of never thought Mike could be my brother. I don't even know how to treat him now. I loved him before I knew he was my brother. There was so much of myself I seen in him, now I know why."

"Don't stress baby everything is going to work its self out," Envy said as she got up and walked over to him then kissed him deeply and passionately. She felt his dick get slightly hard. She grabbed it through his jeans. "I know what'll ease your mind," she said as she got onto her knees and unbuttoned his jeans and pulled them down with his boxers. Then she grabbed his dick and jerked it back and forth. Then with her tongue she let it travel all around the shaft of his dick then taking the tip of it all into her mouth.

"Mmm shit," Michael moaned as the sweet sensation sent chills through his body. She made slurping sounds when her mouth went back and forth taking his entire dick inside her mouth. She moaned as she sucked faster and faster while twisting her head from side to side. Then wrapping her lips around just the tip of his dick and sucking it slowly while moving her tongue around.

"Shit, Envy, baby, that feels too good," Michael moaned as he grabbed the back of her head and looked down at her as Envy looked up and their eyes met.

He began to pump back and forth to a rhythm, fucking her mouth. Envy licked and sucked then deep throated his dick. She pulled back and spit on it and jerked on it real fast. "You going to cum for me daddy, huh, cum in my mouth, baby, cum now," Envy moaned as she stuck out her tongue teasing him.

Michael couldn't hold it anymore between her jerking him off and her sweet sensation of her lips wrapped around the tip of his dick. His toes curled up in the air as he grabbed Envy's hair tighter. "AAHH shit," he moaned as he released and nutted in her mouth. Envy sucked it all up and swallowed it.

Envy stood up with a smile on her face as she took off her jeans and shirt. Michael grabbed her and bent her over on to the dresser and pulled down her thong then spread her ass and slowly let his tongue travel around her pussy lips then thighs. "Mmm," Envy moaned as his tongue traveled to her clit. He licked it up and down than took it into his mouth and began to suck it.

"Whose pussy is this?" Michael said in between sucking and licking.

"It's yours baby, it's yours," Envy moaned while her face lay on the dresser and her ass up in the air. Michael began to suck faster and wildly, then kissing her clit.

"This is some good pussy, my good pussy," he said as his head went side to side with his lips sucking on her pussy lips and clit at the same time driving Envy crazy.

"Damn baby, damn suck that shit just like that, oh my God," Envy screamed as a tear of pleasure rolled down her face. His tongue entered inside her pussy and he moved it all around then his head back and forth as he used his tongue to fuck her. Her toes curled up as she screamed and came hard in Michael's mouth. He stood up and used his forearm to wipe away her sweet juices and slid his dick right into her giving her long deep strokes letting his dick hit her walls. Michael watched Envy's facial expressions as her mouth opened as she moaned with pleasure. He began pounding long and hard watching his dick go all the way in and all the way out.

"Shit daddy, that feels fucking good," Envy moaned while throwing her ass back at him.

"Oh, you want to fuck me back, huh?" Michael said as he lifted one of his legs and put it on top of the dresser letting himself penetrate deep inside her pussy. He began to slam into her as hard as he could. Envy began to scream like a wild animal as she came and he continued to pound away. He held on to her waist. "This is my pussy, my pussy," Michael screamed as he nutted all inside her. Michael pulled out of Envy and she stood up getting off the dresser.

"Damn baby, you were going crazy in my pussy," Envy said while looking at his dark sexy skin covered in sweat and his muscles popping out everywhere making her wetter.

"Yeah and I'm still not done with you," Michael said as he got up on his bed and laid there with his dick pointed straight up in the air. Envy smiled and guided his dick inside of her. She let it fill her insides then laid on his chest. Michael spread her ass cheeks and began to pound real fast teasing and pleasing her pussy.

"Shit! Shit! I'm cumming again, baby," Envy yelled. They spent the whole night enjoying each other's bodies teasing, licking, and pleasing until the sun came up and they fell asleep from being too weak to move.

Chapter 14

Caesar lied in his bed in an abandoned house in East New York, Brooklyn on Hull Street. "Shit, I'm running out of gunmen and I only got four left that's guarding this place all because of fucking Pooky. It's only going to get harder and harder to find more men that's willing to work only for a dream of being rich and taking over Black Ice's business, but it will soon be over. I'll kill Evil then kidnap the little boy and the streets will give word to Black Ice and he will come out of hiding. I'll kill him and get my revenge and then take over the empire that should have been mine ten and a half years ago," Caesar said to himself out loud as he thought up his next plan now that Pooky was dead.

Two of Caesar's gunmen stood downstairs guarding the front door talking while the other two stood upstairs inside a bedroom taking turns having sex with a young pretty crack head girl from down the street. She sucked one dick while the other watched and jerked his dick off until it was his turn. He pulled his dick out of her mouth and bent her over and pushed his dick inside her and began to pound away. The young woman moaned and screamed from the pain. With just one look you could tell she was only sixteen, but with the promise of crack, there was nothing she wouldn't do.

Caesar lay on the bed with his eyes open staring at the ceiling when something in his body told him something was wrong. He learned to always listen to his instincts. He rolled out of his bed and went into his closet and pulled out a black

AK-47. He cocked it and aimed at his bedroom door. "Shit, I know you're here," Caesar yelled. Downstairs the men guarding the front door flew backwards as the front door exploded into pieces. The two guards looked up while on the floor and couldn't believe their eyes as five masked gunmen came through the door aiming an Uzi. They squeezed the trigger, "Oh shit," one of the guards yelled as he rolled just in time and the bullets missed him, but it was too late for his friend as bullets ripped and shattered his body like paper. As he watched his friend die, he jumped up and pointed his gun letting off two shots. The bullets flew into one of the masked gunmen chest sending him flying backwards killing him. The four masked gunmen aimed at their target and sent bullets flying. The guard's body shook as he was filled with holes and he fell forward dead. A masked man stepped out of the shadows. "Go upstairs and kill whoever is left, but leave the leader to me," he ordered.

The four masked men rushed up the stairs. The two of Caesar's henchmen that were in the room stopped fucking the young girl and grabbed their guns. One ran out of the room shooting and hit one of the masked gunmen in his head and chest, but then was filled with bullets himself from automatic fire sending his blood and guts flying everywhere. The last three masked gunmen stood at the bedroom door where they could see Caesar's last henchmen naked with a naked young crack head woman he was using as a shield, while pointing his gun at her. The last of the masked men walked up the stairs and to the door, "Move," he yelled. His masked men moved to the side while keeping their guns aimed at their target. “Get back! Move or I’ll kill the girl,” the henchman yelled while swinging his gun back and forth at the masked men. The leader of the masked men looked at the young woman’s naked body and licked his lips through his mask, “Hmmm.”

“I said stay the fuck back or I’ll kill this bitch,” the henchman yelled again as he noticed that one of the masked men was moving closer.

“You keep talking. Why don’t you shoot the fucking bitch already? I’m tired of hearing your damn mouth,” the lead masked man yelled. The henchman looked shock and didn’t know what to do. “Okay I see you’re taking too long. So I’ll make up your mind for you,” the leader of the masked men yelled then raised his hand and aimed his 44 bulldog revolver and fired. The bullet hit the woman in the shoulder and came out of her back and crashed into the henchman’s chest sending them both flying to the floor. The leader of the masked men then put his gun in the holster and pulled a long melt wire. The henchman was screaming and rolling around on the floor as well as the woman who was bleeding and crying. The henchman tried to reach for his gun on the floor that he dropped when he felt the melt wire wrap around his neck. He struggled and wiggled around, but couldn’t break free. His eyes began to roll to the back of his head as he lost oxygen. His body jerked and he swung his hands and hit the masked men and tried to grab him, but all his efforts went in vain as his body stopped moving and he lost consciousness.

The masked man continued to pull even harder. The harder he pulled the more the melt wire ripped and cut through the henchmen's neck. His body jerked a few more times as the wire cut through his flesh. The other three masked men watched in horror as their leader continued to pull then a sound of a bone breaking and cracking. Then Caesar's henchmen's head ripped off and blood gushed out from his neck, "Grab the fucking head and put it in the bag and one of you take the girl to the van," the leader masked man ordered as he looked down at his work.

The crying woman pleaded on the floor, "Please no, you said you would set me free for good if I did what you told me too, please no more," the woman cried out as one of the masked men picked her up. He threw her up on his shoulders and carried her down the stairs and then out of the house and tossed her into the back of a black van and locked it.

Caesar was sweating out of fear as he held the AK-47 at his bedroom door. He heard the gunshots and his men screaming along with the woman's cries and he knew in his heart they were all dead. He took his left hand and moved his long dreads out of his face and pulled it back making sure not to lower his gun that was aimed at the door. The house was completely dark with no light at all. He hit a button on the AK-47 that turned on a red infrared beam, "Come on, come on," Caesar whispered to himself as he waited. Then he heard a noise for the first time in twenty minutes. He looked and could see the doorknob being twisted,

"AAHHH," he screamed and squeezed the trigger to the AK-47 sending a hail of bullets into the door ripping through it and the wall. "Come on, come on, you'll die before you get your hands on me," he yelled and stopped firing to see if there was any more noise or movement. He squinted his eyes to focus on the door through the dark. The door flew open and he sent a spray of bullets wildly at the figure at the door. When he seen the body drop he aimed at it and continued to fire. A flash of orange light lead up to the dark room Caesar stopped firing to get a good look at the body he was filling with holes that lay on the floor. He looked down to see a naked man's body with no head. He looked up just in time to see another figure at the door and two more that stepped inside to the room, but disappeared into the dark. He aimed at the figure at the door and bullets filled the lungs and heart of the masked gunmen. Caesar stopped shooting and then felt the presence of someone beside him and behind him. He tried to turn around, but was too slow as he felt a strong arm wrap around his neck then a hand with a rag in it wrap around his mouth and nose. He smelled something sweet as he struggled to get free, but then felt weak.

"Go to sleep now boy. You're in my hands," was the last thing Caesar heard as his world went black and he lost consciousness.

Chapter 15

It was Sunday and Michael couldn't be happier. He was dressed in an all tan suit and Mike had on a dark brown one and Envy had on a Channel tan dress with the shoes and bag to match. They all smiled as they hopped into the car and headed to New Jersey. Once in East Orange, New Jersey, Michael drove down Main Street until he pulled up in front of a big church. He found parking and got out of the car with Envy holding Mike's hand. They followed him inside and greeted people as they looked for a seat. Michael quickly spotted his mother and her cousin Janet. He made his way to the front where she was seated, "Hey moms, how are you?" Michael said while kissing her on the forehead.

"I'm fine, baby. God is good and he got you in the house of the Lord to chase that demon out of you."

Michael shook his head, "I can never understand why you always say that mother. There's no demon in me," Michael replied.

"Yes, there is baby. It's in you just like it's in that little boy you and Envy got with you. I warned you about that child. He will bring you problems and death. God has shown me," Rachel stated.

"Mother, I didn't come here for this and please don't say that too loud Mike might hear you. He is just a child and doesn't need anyone telling him he has a demon in him. He has been through a lot just like I have as a child or did you forget?"

Michael said looking his mother in the eyes.

Rachel's mind raced back to all the mistakes she made by smoking crack and how bad it hurt Michael and felt ghetto for it. "You're right baby, but remember I had no choice but to smoke that stuff always keep that in mind."

"Well, that's the past mother and this is the present like you taught me. We're just going to count our blessings day by day." Michael said hi to Janet and she just nodded her head. Janet looked at Michael with hate mixed with fear. All she could see was Black Ice when she looked at him and in her heart she blamed Michael for losing her boyfriend, Jay, the love of her life and because of that she felt she would always be alone. Unknown to Rachel, she dreamt of killing Black Ice and Michael and anyone or anything that has or had a part of Black Ice. She looked at Mike who was now sitting next to Envy and with just one look at him her blood boiled for some reason.

Michael tried not to let his mother's words bother him. It was Mike's first time in church and he loved it from watching the people sing and the pastor tell them God loves them. His heart felt so at ease.

Four hours later, Envy, Michael, and Mike were leaving the church with everyone else and were feeling so good. "Okay baby, where are we going now? I want to go to IHOP. I'm hungry," Envy said as she sat in the passenger seat.

"Okay, that sounds good, but we have to make a stop to my mother's house first."

"Okay, that's not a problem, but remember

I'm eating for two now so you got to feed us," Envy replied.

Michael smiled then stopped and looked at her and she knew she had spoken out loud. They had made a promise to talk to Mike about the baby so he wouldn't worry, but haven't done it yet. Mike stood in the back seat and looked back and forth at Envy and Michael. His good feeling from church had just left him. 'There not going to want me anymore once they have a baby of their own. I'll just be in the way and they'll put me back in foster care and even if they don't, they will treat me different. I've seen how my other foster parents treated me and how they treated their own kids,' Mike thought to himself as he felt as if he wanted to cry and his heart got sad all over again.

Envy turned her head and looked back at Mike and by his facial expressions she knew something was wrong. "Mike, we're going to talk when we get to IHOP so smile for me baby. I love you."

Mike smiled a fake smile not wanting Envy to worry about him, but did feel better by just hearing her say she loved him, "Okay."

"Mike, sit in the car for a second me and Envy are going to speak with my mother and we'll be right back," Michael said. Mike shook his head up and down. Then Michael and Envy got out of the car. Michael took one more look at Mike before he went inside the house. He knew something wasn't right with Mike. "Envy we're going to have to talk to him about the baby at IHOP so he don't worry and think we're going to abandon him. I can see the pain all in his eyes his whole mood switched when you talked about the baby."

"I know baby. We're going to handle it, but what about the other thing. Are you going to tell him?" Envy replied.

"Umm, not yet because I still don't know how to deal with it myself," Michael replied.

"Michael by telling him it will help. He'll know he's a part of this family we're building in a big way."

"Envy, I know you're right, but we'll talk about this later. This isn't the time or place," Michael said as he walked into the living room and Rachel was sitting there still in her church dress. Michael couldn't help to think how beautiful his mother still was.

"This isn't the time and place to talk about what boy. You don't know by now you can't hide nothing from me? God has already shown me everything," Rachel said to Michael.

"There's nothing to hide mother."

"Oh, so now you're going to lie to me," Rachel said while laughing.

'Damn, times like this I swear my mother went mad with God telling her everything. Fuck it, if it keep her clean and off of drugs then God is strange and works in ways I can't see,' Michael thought to himself.

"Michael and Envy sit down next to me the both of you." Envy looked at Michael then sat down on one side of Rachel while he sat on the other. "I'm going to talk to you both and Michael try not to get frustrated like you always do or let my words in one ear and out the next. I know you swear I lost my mind because I tell you the Lord shows me things, but he does. You think you can keep secrets from me, but I'm your mother you think I don't know your father left you a house and you found money in it." Michael's jaw dropped in shock and was about to speak. "Shh, boy I said, don't talk just listen." Michael and Envy both sat there staring at Rachel. "Michael, you must think I'm a fool not to know. How else can a nineteen year old boy buy and own a center? Yeah, you're smart and smart enough to get the government and city to fund you to make it legit, but without that money to get you in the door you wouldn't be able to do shit. I know in your head you're asking how I know about the money and house. I just do and I know your father. He's a bad man. Shit, I think he's the devil in the flesh, but I also know he wasn't always like that. I always used to tell you that as a child even the money I found in one of his stash house's ten and a half years ago to run away and that got me this house. Trust he planned for me to find that shit. He's evil, but has a side that's still somewhat good inside him that loves you and me, but his love is very different. Once I knew you got that letter when you were fifteen from him with the house title, we moved to a different part of New Jersey because I knew he found us, but wasn't ready to come get us. He's waiting, baby, waiting on you. He wants you to be just like him, cold hearted and able to kill at will. But you have me in you and no matter how much of him there is in you, you know to never hurt a woman or child. But him, shit baby, we already know. Michael you still think I'm crazy right?" Rachel said while smiling. "Well I know that Envy here is pregnant," Rachel said as she rubbed Envy's stomach.

Envy's eyes opened wide, "But how, how did you know?" Envy asked. She was surprised and shocked and kind of scared at the same time.

"I keep telling you babies. God shows me some things just like I know that boy, Mike, is your brother Michael. Did you know that?"

"Wait! How the hell did you know that? I just found out my damn self," Michael yelled as his eyes got wider.

"Michael, I knew from the first time I seen him and was surprised you didn't and you been in his life for more than eight months. He looks just like you. He has you and your father's cold eyes and facial features."

"So, that's why you didn't like him? You knew he was the other woman's baby?" Michael asked.

"Yes, and no, baby, I won't lie a part of me didn't like him because of that and reminded me of that woman he started smoking crack with, but after a while I knew I couldn't blame her knowing your father. I can only think what he did to that poor girl, but it's not that I don't like Mike. God sent me a dream that he has more of his father in him than his mother. That he will be the reason behind a lot of you and Envy's problem, but you two won't listen to me. What's in the dark will come into the light, in other words, you will see for yourself."

"Mom, me and Envy won't let him be like

Black Ice. I'm not because you raised me and we're raising him better than that. So, he will always feel love," Michael replied.

"Michael, do you remember the story of the frog and the scorpion?" Michael shook his head no. "Okay, I'm going to tell you and Envy. The scorpion was stuck at the river and wanted to cross, but couldn't or he'd drown. A frog came along and the scorpion asked, 'Mr. Frog can you please carry me on your back across the river?' The frog looked at the scorpion like he had lost his mind. 'Mr. Scorpion, do I look crazy to you? If I carry you across the river on my back, you'll surely sting and kill me,' the frog replied. 'No, I won't Mr. Frog because if I do, I'll drown and die,' the scorpion replied. The frog thought about it for a second and knew the scorpion had a point. 'Okay, Mr. Scorpion, I'll do it, hop on.' The scorpion hopped on to the frog's back and the frog jumped into the river and began to swim. Half way across the river, the frog felt a sting in his back, 'AAHHH, you stung me,' the frog screamed as he began to get weak and sink. 'Why did you sting me, Mr. Scorpion, when you gave me your word, now we're both going to die.' The scorpion's last words were the only ones that came to his heart, 'I couldn't help it. It's in my nature,' was the last thing he said as him and the frog drowned.

"So, what I'm trying to say Michael is you, your father, and that little boy are scorpions because of his blood. No matter what all three of you will sting and kill, none of you will be able to help it. It's your nature and that boy is the biggest scorpion there is."

"Okay, mother I'm tired of you talking bad about Mike. I didn't come here for this. I just wanted to ask if you have new guns for me and Envy. I have some, but the ones you gave us are stronger."

"Michael, you don't need new guns just switch the bullets you were using so police can't trace it, but you can only use them one more time. Once you do that and by then, I'll have some new ones for you," Rachel stated.

"Okay," Michael said while kissing her on the forehead and tried to control his anger.

"I'm good baby and safe. God is protecting me and I'm always ready," Rachel said while digging in her purse and pulling out a 9 mm Taurus with a white pearl handle then put it back in her bag. Black Ice don't know I'm here. I feel it. You need to listen to your instincts, baby."

"Okay mother," Michael said and walked to the door.

"Bye mom," Envy said as she got up and kissed Rachel on the forehead.

Rachel rubbed Envy's stomach. "You stay strong Envy and keep faith and go feed my grandbaby."

Michael and Envy stood outside by the first door with both their minds spinning. "How the fuck did she know all of that?" Michael said out loud.

"Baby, I believe she really do see things and you should listen and remember the things she said," Envy replied.

"Envy, I'm not about to believe some shit

about my father having a nice side to him. If he did, he wouldn't have beaten me so bad. I wished I was dead or beat my mother and make her smoke crack. I'm not listening to my mother talking that scorpion and frog shit."

Envy shook her head. "You need to listen. She knew too much without us telling her about the baby and Mike," Envy stated.

"Envy, we'll talk about this later," Michael replied as he looked at Mike moving around in the back seat looking restless. Michael and Envy hopped into the car and they pulled off heading back to New York and to IHOP.

Janet had her room door half way open and heard everything Rachel had told Michael and Envy. "How in the world could Rachel think that monster has a heart and I knew there was something I didn't like about that little boy? I lost the love of my life and they're acting as if everything is alright. I will get even and kill the demon's bloodline," Janet said out loud to herself as she went up under her bed and grabbed a pump shotgun she kept there for the day Black Ice would return. She held the shotgun in her hand and just stared at it. "Going to wipe the earth of all demons," she said over and over while rocking back and forth.

Mike felt much better. There was something about sitting in IHOP with Envy and Michael that always made him happy as he ate his pancakes with strawberries. He looked up and could see Envy and Michael whispering and looked as if there was a lot on their minds. "Mike, me and Envy got to tell you something. I know you may have overheard that

Envy's pregnant and that means she's having a baby." Mike stopped eating and looked up as his stomach began to hurt.

"Yes baby, I am pregnant, but we don't want you to think we're going to love you any less. You'll be like a big brother to the baby and protect it like you do us," Envy said while taking Mike's hands and holding it.

Mike smiled, "A big brother, I like that," he replied. "Michael, you promise that you and Envy will love me the same and not treat me any different like those mean people in the foster homes I've been in?"

Michael couldn't help but feel bad as he looked at the little boy and all the pain he had been through and never knew love. Michael thought to himself. "Mike, we love you and you're a part of this family and we're not going to let nothing break us apart. We're going to adopt you. See right now in the court's eyes we're just your temporary guardians, but not in our eyes. We're going to fill out the papers Monday to be your permanent guardians."

"In other words, no one can take you from us ever," Envy stated.

"You promise Envy, you really mean it?" Mike asked looking her in the eyes.

"Yes baby, I promise, I mean we promise that no one will ever take you away."

With Envy's words and Michael's love, Mike smiled the biggest smile he ever had in his life and went back to eating. Envy smiled then gave a look to Michael, Michael knew the look and what she wanted him to do. "I'm not ready Envy, but I will be soon," he replied and went back to eating. 'I'll tell him when I'm ready. It's all a little too much for all of us to deal with. There's so much changing that's happening so fast. How am I going to tell him we have the same father and he's my brother? He will ask where I have been his whole life when he was being abused. How do I tell him I didn't even know he was born?' Michael thought to himself as he tried to push the thoughts out of his mind.

Chapter 16

Black Ice looked at Tiffany and Star then at Yasmin chained to the wall and smiled his devilish grin. He pulled a key out of his pocket and uncuffed Tiffany's hand. Then he looked at Star's face and was amazed at the two deep cuts he left on her cheek. Star closed her eyes and her body began to shake as he stood face to face with her as if he wanted to kiss. "HA HA HA," he laughed and grabbed her face then kissed her on the lips. He uncuffed her hands and feet then looked at her stomach that was growing from the baby inside. He walked over to Yasmin and uncuffed her. One of Black Ice's guards came in with three plates of food and a tray full of crack with three crack pipes. "Ladies you know the routine. You get two hours free from your chains to eat and smoke, but first," Black Ice said as he pulled down his jeans and his nine inch dick stood straight up in the air, "Come and please me."

Tiffany felt as if she wanted to throw up as she crawled to him with Star and Yasmin by her side. She took his dick in her mouth. 'Damn I wish I could bite this shit the fuck off,' she thought to herself as she sucked the tip of his dick. Star slowly sucked his balls taking each ball in her mouth one by one then both at the same time. "Shit, that's right, suck that shit you filthy whores." He took his dick out of Tiffany's mouth and stuffed it into Yasmin's and grabbed the back of her head and began to pump fast and hard. Yasmin felt as if she wanted to choke as his dick hit the back of her throat. "Don't you fucking move," Black Ice yelled as he seen her grasping for air. He pulled out and lifted Star's face up and stuffed his dick all the way in with long strokes while Tiffany sucked his balls and Yasmin licked around his private. Black Ice clenched his teeth and pulled out of Star's mouth. "Lift your fucking face up," he yelled. Yasmin, Tiffany, and Star did as they were ordered and he jerked his dick hard and fast pumping it back and forth until he nutted and cum shot out of his dick spraying all onto three women's faces. "Oh shit, that was good," Black Ice groaned as he pulled up his boxers and jeans. He looked at Tiffany wipe the cum off her eyelids and forehead and tossed it on the floor with her finger. "Bitch, are you mad. Pick that shit up and swallow." Tiffany's face balled up in anger. "Tiff, don't make me tell you again." She nervously bent over and stuck out her tongue and let it travel across the floor where cum was and licked it up. Black Ice smirked then looked at Star and Yasmin wiping the cum off their face and putting it in their mouth. "Very good ladies, come here Tiffany," Black Ice ordered. Tiffany stood up barely looking him in the eyes. She walked over to him. Black Ice looked at her stomach that was now poking out and rubbed it. "You're getting big, Tiffany. What are you now maybe four and a half months?"

"Yes, I think I'm four and a half months, but I'm not sure because in this room with no clocks or television. I don't even know what day it is," Tiffany replied as she lowered her head.

"You should have never tried to run and you

wouldn't be in here with the fucking dogs and these bitches. You belong to me personally, and me only, but your damn actions and mouth is what got you in here and what kept you in here. You stay in here for just two more weeks and I'll move you. And I might think about taking your friend with you, but not out of kindness just to keep you in line. For whenever you act up, she will feel pain for your mistakes. Now sit down and eat. I'll have more food sent to you," Black Ice said as he walked across the room to his four hyenas and laughed as he pet them. He unhooked one and held him by a leash. With the hyena by his side, he entered the code for the steel door and it opened. He left and shut the door behind him.

Tiffany and Star both spit out the cum they were hiding under their tongue. "I hate that fucking animal. I swear one day I'll kill him," Tiffany yelled.

"Yeah, I'm with you. Shit, I wanted to bite his dick off," Star replied.

"Hell yeah, you bite his dick then I bite his balls," Tiffany said while eating.

"I could see his face now," Star said laughing and making Tiffany laugh also.

"You both need to stop thinking and talking like that before he hear you and feed you to those damn hyenas across the room," Yasmin said while letting out crack smoke from her mouth. She stuffed the pipe with more crack rocks and held the lighter to it and inhaled the thick smoke.

"Why the fuck do you care you back stabbing bitch and why are you still smoking that stuff? There's no one in the room to force us anymore. Now, it's out on our own free will to smoke it or not. You're pregnant, Yasmin," Tiffany replied.

"Fuck that! I mean, well smoking takes the pain away and makes me forget about being here and I could care two shits about this baby inside of me. Those men raped me repeatedly every day. I don't even know which one of them is the father and I don't care. If I could kill this child growing in me, I would."

Tiffany and Star shook their heads in shame. "You're a counselor for abused women and drugs you should be able to fight the need to smoke that shit. We have, even now it hurts and it calls us. We have to be strong. We can't tell women to be strong every day at work and we can't even do it our damn self and I don't know which one of those evil men got me pregnant. They raped me too over and over, but I'm going to love this baby because it's a part of me. If we ever do get away from this beast, my child will have a good life," Star stated.

Yasmin rolled her eyes and stuffed her pipe with more crack then began to smoke. "You bitches are crazy if you think we're ever going to leave this place alive and I will ever love this child. If I did keep it, it would always remind me of this place and my life is over. Look what the fuck happened to me? I'm a fucking crack head at twenty two and this baby will only be another child of a crack head. Tiffany you shouldn't be shaking your fucking head and judging me. You're the one with the seed of a monster growing inside of you. Shit, you're a fool girl because in his sick mind he loves you. I'd be sucking his dick and fucking him and telling him I love his ass too because I know he had your ass living better than this being chained to a fucking wall in a dark ass room with fucking dogs that laugh all damn night and day that's just waiting for the chance to eat us."

Tiffany jumped up and ran across the room and smacked Yasmin so hard that her head turned and the crack pipe flew out of her mouth. "Who the fuck are you? You're not the same woman I grew up with, not the same friend I loved," Tiffany yelled as she was about to hit her again, but then stopped and watched Yasmin search on the floor until she found the crack pipe and picked up the piece of crack that fell out and tried to stuff them back in. Star and Tiffany looked in amazement their friend turned into a true crack head and that was the only thing she cared about. There was a full tray of crack right by Yasmin, but she was so in love and hooked to the drug, she couldn't bear to see even a little crumb go to waste.

Tiffany walked back to where Star was and sat back down. "Damn, in his mind he does love me, but that's only because he thinks I'm Roxy at times and he won't let none of his other men touch me and this baby is his, but more of mine and I'll love it," Tiffany said out loud to no one in particular. Star saw her friend hurting and hugged her and then held each other crying.

"Don't worry Tiff. We're going to be fine."

"You bitches are really crazy. We're sitting on concrete floors and shitting and pissing in buckets and we're going to be okay?" Yasmin said then laughed while she rocked back and forth and inhaled more smoke from the crack pipe.

"Yasmin, shut the fuck up because I'll do more than smack your ass like Tiff just did," Star yelled. Yasmin got quiet and knew Star's words were more than a threat. She stuffed her pipe with more crack and continued to smoke.

Chapter 17

Caesar woke up in a dark room. He tried to move, but couldn't when he realized his hands were cuffed behind his back and his whole body had been wrapped around in thick chains to the chair he was sitting in. He had his head down and could see he wasn't wearing any shoes and the chair was bolted onto the floor. He lifted his head up and tossed his long dreads to his back that came down to his shoulders. Caesar looked around the room, but couldn't see anything but darkness. Then a large steel door opened. He had to close his eyes from the bright light. He opened his eyes to see two figures and what looked like a dog walking towards him. "So, Caesar you didn't learn from the first time around," a voice boomed. The voice sent chills through Caesar's body he knew it all too well. Black Ice stepped into the light with a machete in one hand and a leash in the other that held his hyena. Then his new lieutenant, Tiwan, stepped by his side. "Tiwan, I want you to meet Caesar. My old lieutenant, Caesar, meet Tiwan, he has your job now," Black Ice said with a smile on his face. "Caesar, Caesar, you're such an ass. You live after I threw your ass in a barrel in the Coney Island Ocean. It's been ten years and you stood on the low in hiding. Why the fuck you didn't stay there?" Black Ice asked with a smirk on his face.

Caesar looked at him in the eyes. It had been ten and a half years since he laid eyes on Black Ice and his heart still pounded with fear. The eyes of Black Ice were still the eyes of a demon. A part of him was hoping on the day he did find Black Ice, he'd be a full blown crack head, skinny, weak, and smoked out, but that was not at all what he was seeing now. Even in his forties, Black Ice was stronger than most men half his age. Muscles popped out everywhere from his body like he worked out every day.

Black Ice had seen the shock in Caesar's eyes. "What you expected me to be some washed up crack head didn't you? You stupid ass. You haven't learned shit from ten years ago just like you thought I was washed up and unable to run. Shit, I saw through you and Ace's plan. To answer the questions that must be running through your mind. Yes, I still smoke crack fool, but I learned how to control it and not smoke as much. I take steroids to keep my weight up and work out every day because I'm waiting for my boy and I have to be ready for when he comes. Speaking about that topic, why the fuck you come out of hiding?"

Caesar knew he was a dead man no matter what. Black Ice had failed once on killing him. He knew there wouldn't be a second time he'd get away. "I'd been waiting and watching for you to show your black face for years to get revenge. You took everything from me, my son. You monster how do you chop up an eight year old boy? So, to get even I decided to kill your son and bring you out of hiding," Caesar yelled.

Black Ice smirked, "So, how did that go, huh, not so easy to kill a child of mine as easy as it was for me to chop your fucking son's head off."

"Fuck you! Fuck You!" Caesar yelled

repeatedly. Black Ice looked at his lieutenant and Tiwan knew what to do in a swift move Tiwan elbowed Caesar in the nose breaking it and sending blood squirting out of it. Then he began to work on Caesar's face and punched him in the eyes then went wild and sent blow after blow to Caesar's jaw and used his face as a punching bag. "That's enough Tiwan." Tiwan stopped and was smiling as he looked at Caesar lumped up face covered in blood and knots. "I bet your ass wished you stayed in hiding," Tiwan said as he stepped back.

Caesar spit up blood before he spoke, "I know you're going to kill me, but I just got to know how you found me?"

Black Ice laughed, "It was easy. First, you kept attacking my son and I'm always watching him in some kind of way, but if he couldn't handle you. He didn't deserve to live and have my blood flowing through his veins. Shit, to be honest, if I didn't get you, he would have found you in time. And how I found you was so easy. That young crack head your men were fucking belongs to me. I promised to set her free for good if she could lead me to you. Of course, I lied and fed her to my hyenas. Caesar, you're right. I am going to kill you, but very slowly and painfully," Black Ice said and raised the machete he had had in his hand and swung with all his might and chopped off Caesar's leg from the knee. "AAHHH," Caesar howled in agonizing pain with blood gushing out of his open wound.

Tiwan passed Black Ice a small bottle. Black Ice opened the bottle and poured out the liquid onto the machete. Then pulled out a lighter and flicked it. The machete caught on fire. Tiwan and Caesar both looked as Black Ice held the machete in his hand with the blade now on fire. When Black Ice was sure enough that the blade was hot, he looked at Caesar then pressed it on the open wound where Caesar's right leg used to be. Caesar screamed and squirmed as the hot blade cooked and melted his flesh. The smell of cooked meat was in the air. "AAHHH," Caesar screamed and tears rolled down his face. When Black Ice was sure that the wound was closed and the bleeding had stopped, he removed the machete that was now smoking and melted and cooked flesh stuck to it. Caesar head was held down to his chin as he felt as if he wanted to pass out. "Don't pass out like a little bitch, Caesar. I want you to see this."

"Fuck you! Fuck you!" Caesar yelled barely able to get the words out. Black Ice chained the hyena to the wall and it began to laugh with excitement. Black Ice picked Caesar's leg off the floor and walked over to the hyena and held the leg over its head enticing the hyena. Blood dripped out of the leg and watched the hyena rip through it cracking the bones and swallowed a large piece of meat.

"You know Caesar, I seen him eat more times than I could count, but it always ceases to amaze me how strong their jaws are and then eating even the bones. Shit, I found the best way in the world to get rid of a body. They never leave any evidence. That's how I'm going to kill you. I think every three days I'm going to chop off one of your limbs and feed it to my pet here. And he's going three days at a time not eating is going to have him go crazy. When you don't have any more arms and legs, I'm going to set him free and see how long it's going to take a starving hyena to eat the rest of you," Black Ice said then laughed. "I burned your leg because I don't want you bleeding to death. I want you to live to watch everything," Black Ice said as he and Tiwan left the room and the steel doors locked behind them.

Caesar watched in horror as the hyena made a meal of what was left of his leg and began to scream. "AAHHH," he screamed for hours knowing he'd never be heard or saved and never leave that room alive.

Chapter 18

Michael had been planning for the festival for a month now and now the big day was finally here. Twice a year he started giving a festival in the streets of Brooklyn right by his center where people from all over would come and eat for free, listen to music, and their kids could play games. There was a contest from everything to who cooked the best Chili to who danced the best. The festival was one of the ways Michael could give back to the community. People from all over would come and support it from the Mayor to the Chief of Police. People donated money and then there were those who had a little more of things they didn't need and they donated clothes and toys for the women and children in the center. Michael couldn't believe this year's turn out. He had to block off four blocks just for the festival and it still wasn't enough. Cops in blue uniforms stood by the road blocks so no cars could get in and the others walked around to make sure everyone was safe. Michael loved this benefit most of all by doing so much to help people the city was always willing to help him. The festival was full of women and men of different ages listening to loud music, drinking, and dancing. Children of all races and ages were running up and down the street to get on the rides that were set up for them. Michael walked around the festival greeting people shaking their hands with Envy by his side. He was dressed in an all black Ralph Lauren suit and Envy had on a red Dolce and Gabbana dress with the shoes to match and a black thin cut jacket. They stopped every now and then to take pictures with everyone. A photographer followed them around and channel seven news team was out filming everything that was going on.

Michael stopped in front of the police chief and shook his hand. "Michael, you know I have to take a picture with you and your lovely lady."

"Sure, Chief Kells," Envy smiled. "You always know what to say to make a woman smile. If you were a little younger, you might just steal me from Michael," Envy said joking around as they posed for the picture.

"Miss Envy, I still got some kicks in me," Chief Kells replied. It always amazed Envy how older men loved to flirt even when they're in their fifties.

"Michael, I took care of that problem you were having with Detective Roy and his partner. I suspended him for harassment and I'm more than sure you won't have to worry about him anymore. He'll learn his lesson. No one should be able to blame you for your father's mistakes. He took lives and you save them. You cleaned up this community pretty good, Michael. And the donuts you send to the precinct every year helps a great deal."

"No problem, Chief Kells. And thank you for your help as well," Michael replied.

"Michael, I still have detectives out looking for your four missing staff members. What were the young ladies' names again?"

Michael took a deep breath. He tried not to worry or think about his missing counselors. They were more than employees, but friends, "Their names are Tiffany, Star, Yasmin, and Jesse and I pray we find out what happened to them. It's been more than five months and still no word or sign from them. Their families call me all the time crying and wondering when are they going to be found or any new information," Michael replied.

"I know Michael and trust we're working on it," Chief Kells replied.

"Ok thank you and enjoy the rest of the festival," Michael said as he wrapped his hand around Envy's waist. They walked around greeting more people. "Michael, you think they're really trying to find them?" Envy asked.

"Yeah, I'm sure and if not I need to put my ear to the streets and listen because there's something going on in Brooklyn. More than a hundred women went missing and some pop back up in a few months cracked out. Women that would never touch drugs a day in their lives, but when they return from where ever they were they're crack heads and half of them are pregnant. They never talk about what they had been through and I know this only because of the few women that come here looking for help and wanting to get clean, but I can only imagine how many are out there that don't want help or it's too late for them because they're so hooked onto the drug," Michael said and his mind flashed back to his mother and how bad she looked and would get when she was smoking crack.

Envy saw the pain in Michael's eyes she held his face and kissed him deeply and passionately. "Baby, don't stress yourself out. Let's get something to eat with me smelling all this food it got me and the baby starving," Envy said and laughed.

Mike was having fun running around with Crystal. She was dressed in the new pink Baby Phat sweat suit Mike had gave her, but Envy bought. For the first time in his life, he felt like a normal kid as him and Crystal rode the merry go round and then ate ice cream and then jumped around in the big trampoline filled with soft balls and surrounded by a soft balloon like case. "Mike this is so much fun," Crystal screamed while jumping up and down.

"I know right, Crystal. Are you my best friend?" Mike asked while jumping up and down and trying not to fall on the other children.

"Yes, I'm your best friend punk and you're mine," Crystal replied then grabbed his hand and they jumped up and down together.

Michael looked and could see Mike playing with Crystal and then seen Envy ordering more food. She was craving tacos and was standing in the line to get four of them. Michael smiled knowing his new family were enjoying themselves and so was everyone else. "I guess free food could do that to people," Michael said out loud and smiled some more. He stopped as he seen a young white man approaching him in a long brown coat. "Hello, Detective Roy. What brings you out here today? You come to enjoy the festival," Michael said as Detective Roy was now standing in front of his face.

"No, you fucking asshole. I came to keep my eyes on you. I know it was you that made the call that got me suspended you little punk. Niggers shouldn't have that much power or be doing as well as you," Detective Roy replied with his face balled up and turning bright red.

"I'm sorry you feel that way and race has nothing to do with who can do good in this world," Michael stated with his devilish smirk.

"Fuck you. My father spent his life trying to catch your father. It ruined his life. My mother divorced him because he was never home and he killed himself. I lost my father because of yours and I know you're a monster just like him. There's been too many victims' body parts chopped up around your community center over the years and no one pays it any mind because they were drug dealers or men that abused women, but I can't prove it. But, I will one day. Your father is wanted for more than sixty murders and God only knows how much more he did over the last ten years since no one has been able to find him, but I'm going to find him and kill him. I'm going to prove they call you Evil for a fucking reason," Detective Roy yelled while pointing his finger.

"Shit, Detective it sounds like you got issues and I kept telling you I'm not like my father. I hope you don't have a wife detective because you'll end up killing yourself just like your father chasing after me and Black Ice."

Detective Roy balled up his fist and swung, but just before his fist could hit Michael in the face two young cops in uniform who stood right there grabbed his hand just before it reached Michael's face and pulled him back.

"Detective Roy, what are you doing? You know you're not supposed to be anywhere near Michael. You're suspended for following him around. Now, are you trying to lose your job over bullshit?" the uniform cop yelled while wrapping his arm around Detective Roy and pulling him away.

Michael smiled as he watched the detective get dragged through the crowd. "I'll find a way to prove to the world, that they're wrong about you and you're just as evil as your damn father," Detective Roy yelled.

"And your just as crazy as yours," Michael shouted back. The uniformed cops lead Detective Roy out of the festival.

"Listen buddy, Michael helps this community and is friends with powerful people because of the work he does. I think it would be in your best interest to leave him alone and wait out your suspension so you can get back to work," one of the uniformed cops stated as they watched Detective Roy walk to his car.

"Fuck him and fuck who he knows. I'll get his ass and his father one day I know it," Detective Roy said as he sat in his car and started it up and took off thinking of ways to find Black Ice and prove that Michael was really a monster.

The festival was coming to an end and Michael couldn't have been more pleased with the outcome. People donated some things for the people in the center, money, clothes, and canned food. Michael smiled as he hopped into his car with Envy and Mike. "Did you have fun Mike?" Envy asked.

"I had a blast. I played with Crystal the whole time and rode all of the rides. She's my best friend now," Mike replied.

"I'm happy you enjoyed yourself Mike," Envy replied while rubbing her stomach.

Michael never noticed the black car that was following them. "I refuse to let you out of my sight. I know you'll lead me to your father. Then I'll get my revenge and respect from everyone," Detective Roy said out loud to himself as he stayed six cars behind Michael following his every move.

Chapter 19

Black Ice sat on the couch in the room he had turned into a luxurious apartment in the warehouse smoking a cigarette mixed with crack. As he turned on his television to watch the news, a young reporter came on and began to talk. "All day today there's been a festival for the community of Brownsville, Brooklyn. The owner of the community center, Michael Ice, Jr., has been helping this community in many ways from housing and feeding women that have been victims of domestic violence and those who got hooked onto drugs. There was free food at the festival and even rides for the children. It was a great day for the Brownsville community with everyone getting along even Chief Kells, Chief of Police, was out here showing his support along with others who donated food, clothes, and money to the center. Who would have thought so much love could come from a community that just ten years ago was owned by the worse drug lord ever, Michael Ice, Sr. or better known as Black Ice? Rumor has it that he killed and murdered sixty people, women and children, but only five were proven and hasn't been seen ever since. No one knows where he is or if he's still alive, but we do know the damage he did to this neighborhood is being replaced by his son. A man that truly is one of a kind."

Black Ice turned off the television with his face balled up with anger. "I think it's time me and Jr's family meet up," he said out loud and then laughed. He picked up his black machete and pressed the code to open the steel door to his room and walked out. He walked down the hall and took the elevator to the first floor and looked around at the women cooking chronic into crack and his men guarded them and others taking the keys of crack to be delivered to drug dealers. Black Ice walked into a room to see his lieutenant, Tiwan, counting money with a money counting machine and wrapping the money in rubber bands and placing them into duffle bags on the floor. 'Yeah, I got to hide more of my money in a different stash house,' Black Ice thought to himself.

"Tiwan, come with me now," Black Ice ordered.

Tiwan looked up from what he was doing to see Black Ice standing there in the doorway with a machete in his hand. "Okay boss, but what about the money?" Tiwan asked.

"Don't worry about it now. No one is going to take it and I have cameras in this room," Black Ice replied with a smile.

Tiwan got up and followed Black Ice to the basement and entered a room. Caesar had been chained to the chair for three days. Between not having food or water, he would pass out every now and then and woke up to see the hyena chained to the wall looking at him while licking his lips. Caesar looked up to see the figure enter the room. "Caesar, Caesar, you're not looking to good there. I think I'm going to have to send a man in here to make sure you get water to stay alive. Guess what my old friend. It's the third day so you know what that means," Black Ice said as him and Tiwan walked closer to Caesar.

"No! No fucking more just kill me already and get it over with," Caesar shouted back.

"Now, Caesar if I do that, what fun will I have? Your pain and suffering gives me pleasure I can't explain."

Caesar looked in Black Ice's eyes. "That's because you're a fucking monster," Caesar shouted.

"Ha Ha Ha Ha," Black Ice laughed. "That I am well it's what the world thinks of me."

Tiwan loosened up the chains and held out his left arm. Tiwan walked over to Caesar and unlocked the padlock on the chains and wrapped the chains halfway off. He grabbed Caesar's arm. "Get off of me you fucking asshole, let me go," Caesar yelled and squirmed, but was too weak to put up a real fight.

"Hold it all the way out, Tiwan," Black Ice ordered.

Caesar tried to get his right arm free from the chain, but it was no use. The chains were still wrapped around it tightly. He wiggled his left, but Tiwan held onto it by his hand and pulled it all the way out. "I was just going to cut it from the elbow, but looking at my hyena over there, I changed my mind. He's going to need a bigger meal," Black Ice said as he smiled and swung at Caesar with all his strength. "AAHHH," Caesar screamed as the machete ripped through his shoulder. Black Ice got angry as his machete got stuck in Caesar's shoulder. Tiwan's eyes opened wide as Black Ice kept trying to pull the machete out, but it was no use. "AAHHH," Caesar cried and howled in pain. Black

Ice put one foot on Caesar's chest and pulled with all his might until the machete became free leaving a huge cut in Caesar's shoulder. It was split wide open and blood gushing everywhere. "You got my machete stuck in your shoulder. Don't you know this is my favorite one," Black Ice yelled as he became more furious and swung the machete over and over repeatedly. "AAHHH," Caesar screamed as loud as his lungs would allow as the machete ripped through his shoulder, like butter, blood splattered all over Tiwan and his face. The look in Black Ice's eyes made him let go of Caesar's arm and step back a little, but that did not stop Black Ice from chopping away. "You should have stood dead I know your ass wish you did, no one fucking crosses me," Black Ice yelled with every swing then stopped.

He grabbed the arm that was hanging from a piece of skin and meat and ripped it off leaving a large wound where Caesar's shoulder used to be. "Hurry up and burn that shit and shoot him up with some cocaine so his ass don't die on me. I have other things to do," Black Ice yelled as he tossed Tiwan the machete and threw the arm at the hyena. The hyena wasted no time to rip through the flesh, sleeve and all. He swallowed huge chunks of meat.

Black Ice left the room and went back to the first floor. He walked into the room where there was money on the table and duffle bags of money on the floor. He grabbed the four bags and went into the parking lot and tossed the bags in the back seat and took off.

Caesar was too weak to scream. His head

bopped up and down, tears ran down his face. Tiwan put gas on the blade of the machete and set it on fire then pressed it to Caesar's wound burning it closed. Caesar tried to scream, but couldn't. Tiwan pulled out a syringe and stuck Caesar in the arm with a needle filled with cocaine, "This should keep you alive for a few more days and I'll make sure you won't die from the pain. I'll send a man to shoot you up with it every four hours," Tiwan stated as he pulled the needle out and walked away.

"He will do the same thing to you in time, trust me," Caesar said in a whisper.

Tiwan turned around and smiled. "No, he won't. I'm not dumb enough to cross him like you," Tiwan replied and walked out of the steel doors shutting it behind him.

Chapter 20

Michael looked at Envy get dressed while he lay in the bed. They had made love throughout the night. "Baby, where are you going?" Michael asked.

"I'm going to go shopping with my sister today."

"Envy, you shop all the time," Michael replied while smiling.

"Shoot, I love fashion. You know that and I work hard for my money. So I should enjoy it."

Michael noticed that Envy didn't put on her shoulder holsters with her twin 40 caliber guns. "Umm, even I think you should take your guns when you go out," Michael stated.

"I got it covered baby. I took the baby 9 mm out the dresser you got for me and it's in my purse. I got the sub nose 3.45 on my leg holster under my jeans and the knife on my left leg. See, how I'm so thick you couldn't even see it, but I'm good," Envy replied.

Michael had to smile because she was right. Even with her tight fitting jeans, he still couldn't see the gun and knife that was strapped under her clothes.

"So, what are you going to do for the day?" Envy asked.

"I'm going to take Mike to the center to spend time with his new best friend and get some work done and then take them out to eat and the movies," Michael replied.

"You're always working baby you should

just pick up Crystal and take her and Mike out and when are you going to tell him?"

"I have to work even if it is the weekend got to make sure things are running right and besides by me talking to one of those women that need help my words might help them and I'm going to tell Mike soon. Don't rush me, baby, just have to tell him on my own time that he's my brother."

"Okay baby, it's your call, but the longer you wait the harder it will be, but enjoy your day. I love you," Envy said as she kissed him and walked out of the room.

"I love you too," Michael shouted.

It felt like time was flying as Envy and her sister Kema shopped on Jay St. in downtown Brooklyn and then the city. "Damn, I think we went in today. I got like ten bags in my car and four in my hands now," Envy said as she walked back towards her car with Kema by her side.

"Envy, you always overdo it when it comes to shopping," Kema replied while laughing, "But, it's getting late. I'm ready for you to drop me off at home so I can play dress up and try on my new dresses and shoes and you can go home to that sexy man of yours."

"Yeah, you're right Kema. It's like seven o'clock and he should be heading home soon. He took Mike and Crystal out to eat and the movies," Envy replied while placing her bags into the backseat. Kema did the same and they hopped into the car and took off. Envy pulled over in front of Kema's building on Nostrand Avenue. "Okay Kema, I'll see you later," Kema looked at Envy like she was crazy.

"What you mean, your ass is going to help me carry some of my bags upstairs to my apartment little sister."

"Damn Kema, they're your bags, but okay."

Two black vans had been watching Envy and Kema ever since they began shopping on Jay St. and now were parked across the street, watching them remove bags from Envy's car trunk and making trips upstairs to her sister's apartment. "Take her now," Black Ice ordered. Tiwan and four other henchmen jumped out the two vans with M16 automatic rifles. "

"Girl is it me or are these bags getting heavy?" Kema said while grabbing another bag.

"Shut up, no one told you to be like me," Envy replied then looked up to see five men armed with M16 machine guns coming across the street. Her jaw dropped, "Kema!" Envy yelled and went to the front door of her car and grabbed her purse off the front seat and pulled out the baby 9 mm. Kema was coming out of her building to grab the last of her bags when she heard Envy scream her name. She looked at Envy, who now had her gun out, aiming at the men that were now in the middle of the street. Kema dug into her purse and pulled out her baby 9 mm. She aimed and squeezed the trigger. The bullet flew out of the gun and crashed into one of the gunmen's lip and came out of the back of his head. He stood there in shock and then dropped to the ground dead.

"Oh shit, these bitches are armed," one of the gunmen yelled while raising his machine gun.

"We have orders not to kill her," Tiwan yelled as he raised his gun as well. "Shoot up the car and spread. Then grab her."

"What about the other girl?" one of the gun men asked.

"Now, her we can kill," Tiwan shouted as they all ran in different directions and squeezed the trigger to their M16 machine guns. A burst of automatic fire went everywhere. Bullets tore through Envy's white BMW and into Kema's building and crashed into four people walking by killing them. Envy jumped down onto the concrete as her car got ripped to shreds. She lifted the hand with the gun in it and fired. Unable to see her target, a bullet hit one gunman in his leg and screamed out of pain and bent over to grab it. Kema took aim and let off two quick shots and they both hit their mark into the gunmen's chest.

"Get that bitch," Tiwan yelled while ducking behind a car and pointing at Kema who was standing at her building door still firing. Tiwan aimed at Kema and sent a hail of bullets into Kema's direction. Kema jumped back into her building as bullets crashed into the glass breaking it and into the wall. "Shit! Shit," Kema yelled as she bent low and covered her head with her hands out of fear.

Envy stopped shooting wildly when she realized they were no longer shooting at her, but at Kema. Kema's screams echoed in her head, "Leave my sister alone!" Envy yelled while she stayed lying on the ground. She aimed at Tiwan's feet that she could see and fired. The bullet ripped through

Tiwan's boot and his flesh as it got stuck in his foot. "AAHHH, fucking women, I'm going to kill them."

Kema stuck her gun out and continued to fire without looking then heard a clicking sound when she pulled the trigger twice. "Oh shit, I'm out of bullets," she said out loud to herself and got up to run when she felt a hand wrap around her neck then got hit on the back of her head. The gunmen dragged her out of the doorway and swung hard hitting her with the back of their machine guns, "AAHHH," Kema screamed and tried to block their blows, but it was no use as she lost consciousness from the hits to the head.

Envy jumped up and fired at one of the gunmen beating Kema. A bullet hit him in the back and he fell forward on his face. "Stop hitting my sister asshole or I'll kill you where you stand," Envy yelled while aiming at the last gunman who was standing over Kema and ready to hit her again with the back of his gun.

Envy's eyes filled with tears as she watched her sister laying there not moving and blood leaking out of her sister's head. He knew Envy would fire on him before he would have a chance to turn around and shoot her. Tiwan slowly crept up behind Envy and walked on his good foot as it was hard to walk on his left foot with Envy's bullet was still stuck in it. He grabbed Envy in a head lock and wrapped his hand over her mouth and nose with a rag in it. Envy tried to break free, but couldn't. She began to feel her head spin and feel weak as she smelled something sweet. Her eyes began to close and her head dropped down. When she opened them halfway and could see the blood leaking out of Tiwan's left foot with the last of her strength seen aimed and fired. "AAHHH," Tiwan screamed as the bullet ripped his foot in half, but he held onto her and refused to let go. Envy's world went dark as she blacked out. "Yo, help me carry her to the van now before the police come," Tiwan yelled at his gunmen who still had his hands up.

"What about this one? I still think she's alive?"

"Forget about her, just help me with this one she's the target," Tiwan shouted. The gunmen quickly helped Tiwan throw Envy into the back of a van and hopped in as they were about to pull off they could hear a voice scream, "Wait don't leave me." Tiwan looked out the passenger's side window to see one of his gunmen trying to crawl to the van.

"Leave him," Tiwan ordered.

"But boss, we can save him. He's only been shot in the back. He can make it," said the gunman that was driving.

"I told you to fucking leave him, now pull off." The driver shook his head then did what he was ordered to. Black Ice sat in a dark blue car watching the whole thing. Once he seen Envy tossed into the back of the black van, he smiled, "Now, my son you will find me and come to me," he said out loud as he pulled off.

Michael had enjoyed his day with Crystal and Mike and dropped Crystal off at the center and was heading home with Mike, but something in his stomach kept telling him something was wrong. He hadn't heard from Envy all day and it was nine o'clock at night and still no call. 'Maybe she's shopping still or chilling with Kema, but let me call her,' he thought to himself then dialed Envy's number, but got no answer. So he dialed it again and still no answer. 'Now, I know something is wrong. Envy always answers when I call. That's our rule to pick up the phone no matter what we're doing.' Mike had started to fall asleep in the back seat of the car, but could tell something was wrong as he watched Michael's facial expressions.

"Michael, what's wrong?"

"Nothing Mike, well I hope nothing," Michael replied. 'Maybe I should call Kema? Yeah, that's what I'll do,' Michael thought to himself. Before he could dial Kema's number, her number popped up on his phone screen. "Hey Kema, I was just getting ready to call you, how's Envy?" Michael began to drive slower as he waited for a reply from Kema and then all he heard was crying. "Kema, what's wrong? Are you okay?" Michael asked as he pulled the car over to the side of the road.

"They took her, Michael. They took Envy," Kema replied while still crying.

Michael's heart dropped and sadness filled his body then was replaced by fear and anger. "Who took Envy, Kema? Who and where are you now?"

"I'm in Brookdale Hospital and some men dressed in all black took my sister, Michael!" Kema yelled and cried at the same time.

"Kema, I'm on my way to you now." Michael made a u-turn with his car. His heart raced and tears ran down his face. Mike rubbed his eyes and could see Michael crying.

"Michael, what's wrong? Are you okay?"

Michael wiped his tears, "Yeah, I'm okay, but I'm going to have to drop you off at the center for a while. I have to make a run to check on Envy and her sister. When I'm done, I'll come pick you up. The counselors will watch you and you'll get to play and talk to Crystal a little longer." Michael drove like a mad man and pulled up in front of the center. "Go ahead, Mike. I'll be back."

"No, I want to come with you. I know there's something wrong, please let me come," Mike replied.

"No Mike, not this time. Now get out so I can go, please."

Mike got out of the back seat with his feelings hurt and couldn't understand why Michael didn't want him to go with him if something was wrong. Mike walked into the community center. Michael knew he couldn't have Mike with him if something was wrong. He knew there was no controlling the anger and rage inside of him that he had been fighting so long in his life. Envy and his mother had been the main reason he had been able to control it and without them Michael knew there was no holding him back.

Michael pulled up in the hospital parking lot and parked then ran inside. He went to the front desk and seen a lady sitting there on the phone. "Hi, I need to know what room Kema Grater is in."

The receptionist looked up Kema's name. "Are you family?" she asked looking Michael up and down.

"Yes, here's my ID. Now, what room is she in?"

"Okay dear, she's in room 301."

Once Michael heard that he took off to the elevator. Once on the third floor, he headed to room 301. There was a uniformed cop standing by her door. "Hi, I'm here to see Kema. I'm Michael Ice, Jr."

"Oh yeah, I've heard great things about you, but yeah you can go in."

"Thank you," Michael replied and stepped into the room and almost wanted to cry. Looking at Kema hooked up to monitors and face swollen up with knots. "Kema, what happened?" Michael asked while holding her hand.

Kema began to cry. "We just got done shopping and Envy was helping me take some of my bags upstairs to my apartment when five men dressed in black with machine guns started shooting at us. I shot one or two. I'm not sure. I ran out of bullets and that's when they got the drop on me and pistol beat me. The last thing I seen before I passed out was one of the men grabbing Envy. They took my sister, Michael."

'Men in black, could they be the same men that attacked me and Envy in the parking lot? Could it be Caesar?' Michael thought to himself. "Kema, what do you remember about the gunmen tonight? Anything that can help us find Envy, please."

"No Michael, I can't, but Envy shot one of them in the back and I found out by the cop outside my door that he's alive and on the second floor with one cop by his room." As soon as Kema said that, Michael eyes lit up. "That's all I needed to hear. I'll be back to check up on you Kema and I will find Envy. I put that on my life," Michael said then kissed Kema on the forehead and left.

Michael jumped in his car and made a quick trip to the secret house in Flatbush. He grabbed what he needed and drove back to the hospital. He walked pass the front desk without the security guard saying anything to him because he was dressed in an all blue nurse uniform. He took the elevator to the second floor and walked down the hallway. Michael turned the corner and could see a police officer sitting in a chair in front of a room reading a newspaper. "That must be the room," Michael said out loud to himself then looked back and forth. He could tell it was late because the hospital wasn't packed. Michael put on a scrubbing mask over his mouth and nose then walked towards the officer that was sitting down. The officer looked up when he felt a sharp pain in his neck. He looked up to see a male nurse sticking him with a syringe. "Hey, what the fuck are you doing?" the officer yelled then grabbed his neck and passed out. Michael was pleased that the drug in the syringe had worked so fast. He took the handcuff keys off the officer's belt and walked into the room. Michael's eyes tightening up as he looked at the thug that was handcuffed to the bed. The thug looked at Michael. "Damn, aren't you kind of big to be a nurse and when did it become cool to be a male nurse anyway?" the thug stated then laughed.

"There's nothing wrong with being a male

nurse or working hard for your money, but I came to give you a shot to help take away any pain you might be feeling," Michael replied as he stepped closer to the bed with a syringe in his hand.

The thug looked at Michael suspiciously. "That's all right I'm not in any pain. The lady nurse came in here not too long ago and gave me something for the pain."

"Well sir, you still have to take this shot," Michael replied and was now standing over him. Michael grabbed his arm and the thug yelled, "No, I said punk. Let me go."

Michael put his hand over the thug's mouth and pushed the needle in his arm. "You're not a nurse. Who the fuck are you?" were the last words the thug mumbled as he passed out. Michael knew he had to work fast. He unhooked the IV and picked the thug up and put him in a wheel chair then strapped him in. Michael pushed the wheel chair making eye contact with no one. He parked an old beat up car that he stole out of the parking lot and tossed the thug in the back seat and pulled off.

Envy's head was spinning as she slowly opened her eyes. "Look she's coming through now," she heard a woman voice said. Envy could now fully open her eyes and she tried to move her hands, but couldn't then realize they were chained to the wall above her head. She turned her head and couldn't believe her eyes. There were three women chained to the wall right beside her and the face of one she knew. "Tiffany, is that you?"

Tiffany smiled. "Damn Envy, it's good to see you, but not under these circumstances."

"Tiffany, where are we at and why are we chained to the wall?" Envy asked.

"I don't know where we are. I know we're still in Brooklyn in a warehouse owned by Black Ice. I've been here for months, not even sure how long."

Envy's mind raced. 'Damn, I've been kidnapped by Michael's father. Shit I pray Michael finds me in time,' Envy thought to herself.

"Tiffany, where are the other three women at? Star and umm I forgot the other two."

"Hey Envy," Star said speaking for the first time.

"Okay, so you're here too, Star," Envy stated. Envy knew Tiffany and Star well from the community center when she went to visit Michael.

"Well, we all were here. Black Ice killed Jesse on the first night we got here," Tiffany replied and began to cry. "And that bitch Yasmin is hanging next to Star." Tiffany spent the next few hours telling Envy about the months she had been trapped in the warehouse and how Yasmin crossed them and Black Ice whole plan to turn everyone into crack heads and get women pregnant to start a new generation of crack babies. The big steel door opened and Tiffany got quiet. "Do what he says Envy or he will kill you," Tiffany whispered then lowered her head.

Envy watched the large dark skin man walk towards her. She had mixed feelings of fear, anger, and excitement. She always wanted to lay eyes on the man that the world say is a monster. Black Ice walked right up to Envy and grabbed her face. "So,

I finally get to see you face to face and see why my son is so weak for you," Black Ice said while still holding her face. Envy first looked at the long scar on his face that Michael told her his mother gave him. Then she looked in his eyes and fear over took her whole body. "You are beautiful. If my son isn't strong enough to fight to keep you, I think I might keep you as one of my sex slaves," Black Ice stated as he pulled a key out of his pocket and uncuffed her hands. He pulled out a glass pipe full of crack and passed it to her with a lighter. "Don't think I won't kill you, Envy."

Envy looked at him in shock. "How do you know my name?"

"HA HA HA HA," Black Ice laughed. "Envy, you're my son's woman. I know more about you than you think. I'm always keeping my eyes out for Evil and now that I have you, trust he will find me with his blood racing and will be ready to show me what kind of man he is. Now, shut the fuck up and smoke the fucking crack now, bitch." Envy nervously put the crack pipe to her lips.

'Damn, if I don't do this shit, I know he will kill me,' she thought to herself and flicked the lighter on and held it to the end of the pipe and pulled on the smoke and let it out.

Black Ice smirked then with all his might smacked Envy so hard, she hit the floor. "AAHHH," she screamed and rubbed her face then looked at him with hate in her eyes. She wanted to flip on him so bad an call him all kind of names, but her eyes met with Tiffany's, who was shaking her head no as if she could read Envy's mind. Tiffany moved her lips without saying a word. Envy read her lips that said, “He will kill you.”

“Bitch, you think I lived this long because I’m a fool? I said smoke the crack, now put that shit to your lips and you better inhale the fucking smoke this time before I lose my patience and feed you to my hyenas over there,” Black Ice yelled then pointed to his pets across the room that Envy had noticed for the first time.

Envy held the pipe to her lips and lit the lighter and inhaled the crack smoke. She was pissed that the first time she had faked smoking it and it wasn’t good enough to fool him. Black Ice stood over her for an hour refilling her glass pipe with more crack and watching her smoke while he smoked a cigarette mixed with crack. His dick got hard as he watched Envy’s lips wrap around the glass crack pipe. “Stand up and let me see what you got that drives my son so crazy.”

‘Oh please, don’t let this monster rape me,’ Envy thought to herself as she stood up and her head spun from the crack she was smoking and her body felt numb. Black Ice looked at Envy thinking her voluptuous body and let his hand roam on her breast then her ass. Envy’s eyes opened wider as she realized she still had the 3.57 sub nose magnum strapped to her inner right thigh and the five inch knife strapped in the holster to her left thigh. ‘Damn, if he pull down my jeans, I’m fucked, he’ll find it,’ Envy mind raced then she remembered something Rachel told her and Michael. That Black Ice was the devil, but in his sick way he loved him and was just waiting on Michael to be just as evil as him. Then Envy mind rushed to the conversation she had with Tiffany. How Black Ice treated her bad, but not as bad as the other women because she's pregnant and looks like Roxy. "Wait you can't fuck me," Envy yelled.

Black Ice smiled his devilish grin while he unbuttoned her jeans, "Just watch me, bitch."

"No, you can't I'm pregnant with your grandchild."

"What? You're pregnant, if you're lying to me. I'll chop your leg off."

"I'm not lying, it's true. I'm about two and a half months."

Black Ice unbuttoned Envy's jeans and felt on her stomach and felt the knot in it and knew she was telling the truth. He just stared at her and then punched the wall. "Fuck!"

Envy buttoned back up her jeans. "I may not be able to fuck you because you're carrying my grandbaby, but get on your fucking knees," Black Ice ordered and he pulled out his nine inch hard dick. Envy looked at Tiffany, Star, and Yasmin who was still chained to the wall. "Don't fucking look at them. They can't help you now."

Tears rolled down Envy's face as she got on her knees and took his manhood into her mouth. Black Ice grabbed the back of her head and pumped it back and forth. "Yeah, suck it you bitch," he groaned. After a half hour and he still hadn't come. He knew something was wrong. "Get off of me, don't touch me." He grabbed Envy by the hair then cuffed her hands back to the wall. 'Why the fuck I couldn't bust a nut,' he thought to himself. He looked at Tiffany then Star with anger in his eyes. "I'm not getting weak," he yelled then walked over to Star and lifted her legs and moved her panties to the side and ran his dick straight inside of her. "AAHHH," Star screamed in pain as he pounded away as hard as he could go and her hands still chained to the wall and him pulling her from it. "I'm not weak, I'm not weak," Black Ice yelled over and over. As his long dick Star, spreading her legs then putting them on his shoulders and pounding away like the beast he was. "AAHHH," Star continued to scream in pain as she felt his dick all the way in her stomach and hitting her baby. "My baby," Star screamed and cried. Her pain and tears only excited him even more. He smirked and pounded fast as he could then came all inside of her. When he pulled his dick out, it was covered in blood. Star hung from the wall, weak, barely able to stand and in pain. "You hurt my baby," Star said in a weak voice. Tiffany and Envy both were now crying as they looked at Star. "Don't worry, you'll be okay bitch. I'll send a guard in here to set you free for an hour or two so you can clean yourself up," Black Ice said then walked to the steel door, punched in the code, the door opened, and he left.

"Star, are you okay? Is the baby okay?" Tiffany asked.

"I don't know, Tiff. I'm in so much pain, but we'll pray okay," Star replied while still crying hysterically. A few seconds later a guard came into the room and uncuffed the women and left food and crack. Envy and Tiffany helped clean up Star then Star fell asleep in Tiffany's lap.

"You was smart Envy for telling him you were pregnant. So he won't rape you," Tiffany said while rubbing Star's head.

Envy looked at Yasmin in the corner smoking crack and got mad at the fact she didn't even try to help console Star. Then she remembered what Tiffany told her how they ended up in this room. Envy moved in closer to Star and Tiffany. "I just didn't tell him I was pregnant so he wouldn't rape me. I got a surprise for his ass, but first we need to make a plan and you got to tell me about all the doors you remember," Envy said while whispering in Tiffany's ear.

The thug that worked for Black Ice head was spinning. The last thing he remembered was a male nurse holding his mouth and stuck a needle in his arm. He slowly opened his eyes and felt pain all over his body, worse than him being shot in the back, like he was. He noticed he was hanging in the air then looked at his arms. Then screamed, "AAHHH, oh shit, what the fuck is going on here?" he yelled as he could now see small and big metal hooks in his skin holding him up then realized the pain he felt on his back and the back of his legs was from the hooks. He tried to move, but couldn't control his muscles. He looked around and couldn't believe his eyes. There were body parts hanging from hooks all over the room from heads, to arms, and a man's chest. "What the fuck is this?" he screamed and wanted to cry.

"Good, I see you're the fuck up now," Michael said while waiting in the room with a brown book bag.

"Who the fuck are you and why can't I move? Get me the fuck out of here," the thug screamed.

"You can't move because I gave you a drug, but you will be able to feel the pain you're about to receive," Michael replied then opened the book bag and pulled out a black case. He opened the black case to reveal chrome needles seven inches long and some smaller and thicker. "Now, listen I have more than a thousand of these needles here and it's up to you if I use them all. I'm going to ask you a few questions. The first one is where is my woman? The lady you and your friends took?"

"Fuck you, punk I'm not saying shit. You won't get anything out of me," the thug yelled.

Michael smiled and for some reason chills went through the thug's body. The only time that happened was when he looked into Black Ice' eyes or seen him smile. Michael looked at the thug's naked body up and down. He put on black gloves then grabbed his dick and pushed a needle into his ball sac blood squirted everywhere. "AAHHH," the thug tried to move, but he couldn't. He wiggled and squirmed and the more he did the hooks in his back, arms, and legs ripped pulling his flesh causing more pain. Michael took a thin needle and pushed it into the hole of the thug's dick head. He made sure he pushed it in as far as it could go. "AAHHH," the thug screamed and cried in agonizing pain and couldn't believe that Michael was still smiling while pushing more needles into him. Michael took the seven inch needle and grabbed the thug's thigh and forced the needle through it until it came out the back of it. Michael spent the next half hour sticking needles into the thug's lower half of his body. The thug felt as if he wanted to pass out, but couldn't because of the drugs Michael gave him. There were more than seventy needles in his lower half of his body. "Now, I'm going to ask you once more where my woman and why did your men take her?"

"I can't tell you. He'll kill me," the thug replied while crying.

This only angered Michael more. "What the fuck you think I'm going to do to you, but very fucking slow," he yelled then pushed a needle in the thug's left eye. "AAHHH, shit, please stop, stop," He cried out with anger. Michael went to work sticking needles through his chest and arms. "Now, tell me where she's at. Tell me," he yelled every time he stuck a needle into the thug.

The thug couldn't take it anymore. An hour passed and he was feeling pain like he never felt. "Black Ice took her he sent me and some man to get her. I don't know why we always grabbed women, but this one was different that he ordered. We were warned not to hurt her. Usually we can shoot the women and it won't matter, but I overheard she had something to do with his son." As soon as the words left the thug's mouth, it all became clear to him. He looked at Michael with his right eye and for the first time he understood how a man could cause another man so much pain. "You're his son. You're the son of the devil. I see it in your eyes."

Michael stood back as his mind raced. 'My father took her, but why? He knows she's my woman and that means he's going to want me to look for him.' Michael looked at the thug who had needles stuck in all over his body. Blood dripped down to the floor, "Now, motherfucker, tell me where they took my woman? And I might let you go."

The thug looked at Michael with the only eye he had left and laughed. "Are you going to kill me if I tell you or not? You're just like him. The only thing I fear is him more than you because you may kill me, but if I was to go free and he found out I talked. He'll do more than just kill me, but he'll kill my family."

Michael got furious, "What the fuck do you think I will do?" The look in Michael's eyes was the look of a mad man as Michael grabbed his face and pushed a needle through his cheeks making it go through his mouth and out of the next cheek. "Tell me where they took her," he yelled as he stuck more needles into the thug. Michael spent the night sticking needles in the thug and most of the morning until the man died without telling him where to find Envy. Michael looked at the dead thug's body filled with hooks and needles and pulled out a machete and began to chop it up. "I'll find her. I'll find her without anyone's help," he yelled with each swing he made to the body cutting it up into small pieces.

From what Envy was told, this was one of the nights when the black vans left to set women free and they grabbed more women off the street and tonight was just that night. "Envy, you sure this will work?" Tiffany asked.

"Yeah, we planned it all day. And I trust

you. You know what you're talking about. So, trust me the way that I trust you, alright?" Envy whispered to Tiffany.

The street doors opened and shut as a guard walked in with three trays of food. "Okay ladies, this is the last meal for the night," he said as he put the trays on the floor. "I'll be back," he left and then returned with a small plate full of crack and a glass pipes. He pulled the key out his pocket and uncuffed Envy's hands first then uncuffed Tiffany's hands from the wall and then walked over to Star. The guard began to feel up on Star's body, "Hmmm, you still got a nice body even thicker than the first time I touched you and fucked you."

Star looked into the man's face, but barely remembered it. From the look on her face, he could tell she didn't recall him. "Oh, I'm the one that first fucked you when you got here and then the other men took their turn"

Envy quickly unbuttoned her jeans and pulled them down halfway and pulled out the Sub nose 3.57 Magnum from the holster and then pulled the five inch knife out of the holster on the left leg and passed it to Tiffany while the guard was busy feeling all over Star.

He uncuffed Star, "Yea since, you don't remember me. I'm going to fuck you and remind you. Besides, that baby you carrying could be mine."

"But wait, Black Ice said that none of us is supposed to be touched by any of his men."

"Fuck, he won't know. He's out with most of the men selling weight of crack and grabbing fresh meat. I mean, girls," the guard said while smiling putting his finger up inside Star's pussy. Then he felt the barrel of a gun on his temple. He slowly reached for his gun when he felt a knife press against his neck as well. He put up his hands.

"Don't fucking move!" Envy ordered and pulled the 9mm out of his holster and passed it to Tiffany. Tiffany then removed the knife from his throat and then cocked the gun and aimed it.

"What the fucks going on? And how the fuck did you get a gun? " The guard asked with his hands up and a confused look on his face.

"Just shut the fuck up and get back to the wall and keep your hands the fuck up," Envy yelled, "Tiffany pass Star the knife. Star, cuff his hands to the wall," Envy ordered.

Star slowly walked toward him with the knife pointed. She cuffed his right hand up on the wall and grabbed his left hand to do the same when he broke free of her grip and grabbed her by the neck. He then turned her as a shield. "Uncuff me, you bitches or I'll snap her neck!"

"Let her go now!" Tiffany yelled aiming her gun with Envy doing the same, but knew she didn't have a clear shot with Star in the way. "I'm not going to tell you…" Before the words could leave her mouth Star swung the knife with all her might and stabbed him in his stomach. "AHHH!" he howled in pain and let her go. Envy quickly grabbed his loose hand and cuffed it to the wall and then went into his pocket and took out his keys, but was looking for a phone, but had no luck.

"You fucking bitches won't get away with

this when Black Ice finds out you tried to run you'll be dead!" He yelled in pain while blood oozed out his stomach.

"No you asshole. He's going to kill you because we got away. What should we do about Yasmin? Leave her or take her?" Envy asked looking at Star and Tiffany.

A big part of Tiffany wanted to say leave her it was because of the two women that lost their lives, but Yasmin was her childhood friend. "If you talk when you're not supposed to, or give us away in anyway, I'll shoot you in the head myself," Tiffany said as she uncuffed Yasmin's hands and feet.

"Tiff, I think you're crazy and should've left that bitch there!" Star yelled as all four of them made their way to the steel door.

"Tiff, you sure you know the code to open the door?" Envy asked.

"Yeah, I know it. I know Black Ice didn't change it because these fools he got working for him would get too high and wouldn't remember it," Tiffany said then punched in the code. She had seen Black Ice put it in so many times. The steel door popped open and Envy peeped her head out and looked both ways down the hallway. She could see that there were more steel doors and then the elevator came on. "Let's move," Envy said and walked into the hallway with Tiffany, Star, and Yasmin following as they passed the first door they could hear women moaning and screaming and could see thick smoke come from under the door.

"That's the room they keep all the women

in. The guards are probably raping the woman they hadn't set free," Star said in a whisper as they passed the second they heard a man scream as loud as he could "Kill Me! Just kill me already, please!"

"We should open the door and help him," Star said.

"No, we don't have time to do that. We have to worry about ourselves first then we can help someone else," Envy stated as they got closer to the elevator they could see the light on it coming on. "Oh shit, someone's coming!" Envy yelled. "Follow me!" They ran through a door.

"This must be the staircase that leads to all the floors," Tiffany stated.

Envy looked through the glass window of the door and could see three henchmen pushing a group of women about seven in all into one of the rooms. "We have a problem. We need to move faster and get the fuck out of here. They're starting to come back with the women now and all we need is Black Ice to pop up and check that room, then we're really unlucky. Tiff, you said all we needed to do is get to the first floor and the exit to the parking lot is right there."

"Yeah Envy, I'm sure this time around. I know in my heart the first time, but listen to some else," Tiffany said sarcastically and looked at Yasmin.

"Come on, let's move," Envy replied as they walked up the stairs. Envy looked through the glass window of the door on the second floor to see a guard with his back turned leaning on it. "Psst, pass me the knife and hold this," Envy said to Star and passed her the gun and took the knife. "Damn, I only seen this shit in the movies. I pray it works," Envy said out loud to no one in particular. She took a deep breath then opened the door and grabbed the guard wrapping one hand around his mouth then pulled his head back and stabbed him in the neck repeatedly over and over. The guard had no time to react. "Quick, help me drag him in," Envy said as the guard leaned on back her and he held his neck as the blood poured out of it. Tiffany and Star helped Envy pull the guard into the staircase. He lay there on the floor. His body shaking and jerking as all the blood rushed out of his neck then he stopped moving and died with his eyes open looking up at Tiffany, Envy, and Star. "Come on, we have to keep moving," Envy stated as she bent down and took the Uzi off of his shoulder and used his shirt to clean the knife. Envy opened the door and walked out followed by the rest of the women. They took turns creeping by a large room that they could see women naked and cooking crack and cocaine. A few men were guarding them.

"Okay Envy, you see that door on our left down the hall that's our way out of here," Tiffany stated. As they made their way to the door, they heard the elevator sop on the first floor.

"Oh shit, fast in here," Envy said opening a door on the right and they ran into a small room. She peeped out of the door and could see Black Ice talking to his lieutenant, Tiwan.

"We grabbed a lot of women tonight. So let's go have fun with them. That'll kill time until the rest of the vans come back with my money from selling the keys of crack," Black Ice said to Tiwan. 'And after that I'll visit Caesar and then my Roxy, I mean Tiffany whatever,' Black Ice thought to himself as he took a quick look at the workers cooking cocaine and got back on the elevator with Tiwan by his side heading to the basement.

Star turned around in the room and had her mouth opened in shock. There were stacks of money on top of stacks of more money on a table next to a money counting machine. She seen the duffel bag on the floor and unzipped one, "What the fuck, Tiff? You need to look at this?"

Tiffany and Yasmin then Envy turned around and stood there shocked. "Yo, I'm taking one of these bags," Star stated and picked up one of the duffel bag and put it on her shoulders.

"Me too," Yasmin said and unzipped a bag then looked at the money and zipped it back up.

"Are you two going fucking crazy? We're trying to escape and you two are worried about money? I don't know about you, but my life means more to me and the money will only slow us down."

"Fuck that Envy. You don't know how these men treated us, raping us every day and forced us to smoke crack and suck their dicks. Shit, even Black Ice made you do that shit and you don't think we deserve to take something from these evil fuckers?" Yasmin replied.

Envy looked at Tiffany as Yasmin's words rolled around in her head and the flash back of what Black Ice had made her do brought tears to her eyes. "Their right. Fuck that, they hurt us, let's hurt them where it matters to them the most," Envy replied and grabbed a duffle bag and Tiffany did the same.

"Shit, this money could be used to take care of my baby," Star stated.

"Okay, that's enough about the money. Everyone got a bag? Now, we need to get the fuck out of here. The exit is right across the hall. I'm going to peep my head out then we're going to make our move. Is that clear?" Envy stated. The other three women shook their heads up and down.

Down in the basement, Black Ice had the new women already knowing the rules and they smoked crack out of the fear of dying and now his men were taking turns raping them. Black Ice walked out of the large room the steel doors shut behind him. "Now, I just need the rest of my men to come back with my money and more women, but until then I will kill time with that good sweet pussy, Tiffany, and fuck around with my son's girl," he said to himself then burst out laughing. He walked down the hallway and stopped at the first door on his right. He entered the code and the door popped open. "My lovely ladies, I think I'm in the mood to fuck all of ya'll brains out," he said out loud. Then looked at the wall and could only see his guard chained to it bleeding. "No! No!" Black Ice screamed then stomped towards the guard. "Where are they?" Black Ice screamed grabbing the guard by the neck.

"Boss I'm sorry. They had a gun and got the drop on me and stabbed me."

Black Ice face balled up with anger. He looked down at the guard's stomach and seen the blood gushing out from it. He took three fingers and stuffed them inside of the wound. "AAHHH, boss I'm sorry, AAHHH," the guard screamed.

"How long ago did they get out of this room?"

"It's been longer than fifteen minutes," the guard screamed.

Black Ice pulled his fingers out of the guard's wound. "Good that means they couldn't have gotten far," Black Ice said out loud to himself and walked across the room to his three hyenas and unchained them from the wall. "Come on follow me," he ordered the hyenas.

"Boss, what about me? Let me help find them," the guard moaned.

"Oh yeah you, I almost forgot about you. You two come with me and you go eat," Black Ice said as he pointed to one of his hyenas. The hyena turned around and looked at the guard chained to the wall then laughed as it ran toward him and ripped into the guard's stomach and swallowed large chunks of meat.

"Boss, no, no, boss no," the guard screamed as Black Ice left the room with two of his hyenas by his side and left the guard to be eaten by the third one.

"Let's go now," Envy whispered as she opened the door and peeped out and seen no one. They ran out of the room and across the hall. Tiffany entered the code. "Hurry up," Envy said while keeping her eyes down the hall with the Uzi aimed. Tiffany entered the code, but the door didn't open.

"Shit, it won't open, but there were two codes I've seen him use. I'm going to try the next one now," as soon as the words left Tiffany's mouth they heard the elevator stop.

Envy's eyes opened wide as she looked down the hall and seen Black Ice get out of the elevator with six men and two hyenas by his side.

"Tiffany, get the fucking door open now," Envy yelled.

Black Ice turned his head to the left and smirked. "Get them. I want them alive," he said to his men and they ran towards the women down the hall.

"Tiffany the door now," Star yelled with fear in her voice.

"I almost got it," Tiffany replied.

Envy raised the Uzi she took from the guard she killed and squeezed the trigger. A hail of bullets were let out and ripped through two of them. The other four men jumped out of the way into a room in the hallway.

"Boss, they have guns we need to shoot to kill," the henchmen yelled as they pulled out their guns.

"Don't kill them. Shoot them in their legs. If you kill them, then you die. If they get away, you will die," Black Ice screamed.

"I got it," Tiffany yelled as she entered the code and the door popped open. The cool night air hit their faces.

The henchmen in the hallway ducking got scared once they seen the door open to the parking lot and they started firing.

Star took aim and squeezed the trigger of the sub nose 3.57 and the bullets tore through the walls and hit a henchman in the neck killing him.

"Go, go!" Envy yelled following Tiffany out the door. Star followed and Yasmin was the last one out. The heavy duffle bag slowed her down. She smoked more crack than any of the other women and it made her skinny and weak. Envy looked around the parking lot and could see seven black vans and two cars. She went from van to van and opened the door to find the keys, but with no luck.

Black Ice looked at his three dead men and knew he had to handle this himself as ten more of his men ran from different floors to where they heard the gunshots. "What's going on boss?" one of them asked.

"Nothing, follow me and don't kill unless I tell you to."

Envy saw a gate open to the parking lot and a van pulled in. "Tiffany, we're making our move now," Envy said as they crept up to the side of the van as it entered the parking lot. The driver of the van stopped as a bullet hit him in the head killing him. Envy swiftly opened the van door to see a henchman in the passenger seat with an Uzi pointed at her. He looked at Envy as she smiled as he started to squeeze the trigger, but his head exploded like a melon. Tiffany had stood at the passenger side window with her gun still raised and smoking and Tiffany was breathing hard. "Tiffany, grab his body and drag him out of the van," Envy yelled snapping Tiffany out of her state of shock. Envy grabbed the dead henchman's body on the driver's side and pulled him out and Tiffany did the same to the henchman on the passenger side. They hopped into the van that was now soaked in blood. Envy wiped the splattered blood off of her face so she could see better. "Come on," Envy screamed at Star and Yasmin who was ducking behind a car close to the warehouse. Star and Yasmin jumped up with their duffle bags on their shoulders and took off running. As soon as they did, Black Ice busted through the parking lot door with his hyenas by his side and eight henchmen running out.

"Get them, I want them alive," he yelled while pointing his finger. The henchmen and the hyenas took off running.

"Shit," Star yelled as she seen his hyenas chasing her. She stopped running and aimed at one of the hyenas as it jumped up in the air. She fired four shots. The bullets blew large holes in the hyena's chest and blew off half of his face. The hyena dropped to the ground and his body squirmed around as it died. Star took back off running.

"No, that bitch killed my pet. I'll kill her," Black Ice yelled as his eyes opened wide. He raised his 44 bulldog revolver and the first bullet ripped through Star's duffle bag and then her back and then her right breast. She screamed as she fell forward. Yasmin looked back at Star on the floor moaning in pain and smiled and kept running until a bullet tore through her thigh and she stopped and screamed in pain as she hit the ground. The hyena ran to where Yasmin was laying and started chewing on her open wound. "AAHHH," Yasmin yelled and cried as the hyena chewed away.

"We have to help them," Envy yelled as she jumped out of the van with Tiffany by her side. She aimed at the warehouse parking lot door that Black Ice and his men were standing and sent a hail of bullets from her Uzi that ripped through the faces and chests of five men as Black Ice and some of his henchmen jumped back inside the warehouse, just before they could get hit. "Grab them now, Tiff," Envy yelled while still keeping her gun aimed at the warehouse door.

Tiffany looked at the hyena that ripped chunks of flesh out of Yasmin. "I should let him eat your ass for leaving Star back there." She aimed her gun and squeezed the trigger four times sending bullets slamming into the hyena's head and killed it. Yasmin used the little bit of strength she had and pushed off of the hyena's dead body.

"You bitch! You should of killed him sooner and fuck Star if it was her who seen me fall she would of kept running too," Yasmin shouted.

Tiffany shook her head out of shame and couldn't believe this was the same woman that was once her best friend. Tiffany ran over to where Star was laying. "Star, can you move? Are you okay?" Tiffany asked with tears in her eyes.

"Yeah, I can move, but it hurts like hell, Tiff," Star replied while crying.

Tiffany lifted Star up. "Tiffany, grab the money."

"What you still worrying about the damn money?" Tiffany replied.

"Yes, Tiff just grab the shit." Tiffany

grabbed the bag and held Star up with one arm.

Black Ice stood ducking inside the warehouse by the door and was furious as he looked at one of his henchmen. He aimed his gun at one of them and squeezed the trigger and the 44 bullet blew off his face. His other henchmen looked in horror. “Whoever don’t get the fuck out there and stop those bitches from getting away, I will kill them where they stand. I don’t give a fuck if they got guns!”

The henchmen looked into the eyes and seen the devil and knew it was run outside and pray they don’t get shot or die by the hands of Black Ice. They looked at each other and ran out of the door.

Envy saw the henchmen running out like roaches from the warehouse. She aimed and fired and hit two of the henchmen, but the others spread out and started firing at her. “Tiffany and Star, hurry the fuck up,” Envy yelled as an idea popped in her head. “Shit, even if we get in the van and drive off, they’re just going to chase us,” with that thought in Envy’s head she aimed at the vans and cars in the parking lot that the henchmen were ducking behind and fired sending a hail of bullets to the vans and cars. The bullets tore through the gas tank of four vans and then a loud explosion was heard as the vans blew up and sent Envy flying in the air backwards and killing some of the henchmen. Envy got up and squeezed the trigger again and aimed for more vans, but heard a clicking sound. “Oh shit, I’m out of bullets, we got to go,” Envy yelled as she ran back to the van.

Tiffany held Star up and they hurried to the

van. "Wait don't leave me, bitch, help me," Yasmin yelled while laying on the ground reaching out to Tiffany and Star and her leg gushing out blood.

"I'll come back for you," Tiffany yelled as she looked back and seen more henchmen come out of the warehouse firing their guns, but couldn't see because of the smoke from the vans and cars on fire. Tiffany and Star were now sitting in the front seat of the van next to Envy. "Wait Envy, don't go. I have to go back for Yasmin," as soon as the words came out of her mouth, bullets crashed into the van as henchmen were running towards them shooting.

"We can't we have to go now or we won't be able to help ourselves ," Envy yelled as she stepped on the gas and made a big u- turn and drove through the parking lot gates and down the road.

"No, no, don't leave me, don't leave me!" Yasmin yelled as she cried and her words echoed through Envy, Tiffany, and Star's ears.

Black Ice walked out of the warehouse to see some of his men barely moving on the ground as they died from the explosion of the car and vans. Then he looked at his two dead hyenas and grew even angrier.

"Boss, they got away. What you want us to do?"

Black Ice looked at the henchmen with an evil glare. "Fucking follow them and bring them back," he yelled.

"Boss, we can't. They blew up all the vans and cars and the ones they didn't, the tires are shot out. We have to wait until the other vans come back boss," the henchmen said as he stood there shaking with fear.

"No," Black Ice screamed then aimed his 44 caliber revolver and squeezed the trigger sending a bullet through the henchman's mouth and came out of the back of his head. "The rest of you grab that bitch on the floor and clean this place up. We have work to do," Black Ice said as he pointed at Yasmin.

Yasmin laid her head down and cried uncontrollably. "Why? Why did they leave me," she cried as loud as she could as she felt the men grab her legs and dragged her back into the warehouse.

Envy sped down the street as she read the signs and realized where she was at. "We're in East New York by Flatlands and where all the other warehouses and factories are."

Star began to cough up blood. "Hold on Star, we're going to get you help, just hold on," Tiffany said as she held Star and watched her blood pump out fast. "Envy we got to get her to a hospital and fast," Tiffany said while crying at the thought of losing her best friend in the world was more than she could bear.

"Don't worry, Tiffany. We'll get her there. She'll be okay," Envy replied. Then in the back of the van they could hear crying and knocking on the van's door.

"What the fuck is that?" Tiffany yelled.

"I don't know, but we're going to find out." Envy pulled the van over by the side of a house. "Tiffany, give me your gun and you take Star's and come with me to open the back of the van."

Tiffany did what Envy said and they hopped out of the van and with their guns aimed. They made their way to the back of the van. Envy grabbed the door handle and looked at Tiffany and shook her head to let her know she was ready. She pulled the door open fast and aimed into the darkness of the van to see five women crying.

"What are you going to do with us?" one asked.

Envy and Tiffany lowered their guns. "Oh shit, nothing sweetie. We just saved you as well as ourselves. Please get out of the van ladies and make your way home to your families. We have a friend that's badly hurt and we don't have time to waste."

The five women looked at Envy crazy at first then smiled as they climbed out of the van. "Thank you, thank you," they all said.

"Go to that house, knock on their door, and tell them what happened. Call the police and your family. I'm sorry I can't be more of a help, but I have to go."

"Thank you, I hope your friend is okay," the women yelled as Envy and Tiffany jumped back in the van and pulled off.

"Those women don't know how much pain and suffering we saved them from," Tiffany stated as they pulled up into the ER at Kings County Hospital.

"Help us, help us please," Envy and Tiffany yelled as they carried Star into the emergency room.

Doctors came out and helped lay Star on a

gurney and rushed her into an operation room. "Can I come in," Tiffany asked.

"No Miss, she's going to be okay, but you have to let us work. You're only in my way," one of the doctor's replied.

A half hour later, a doctor came out and asked about Star and told Tiffany and Envy that Star and the baby would be alright, but can't be seen. She was sleeping from the medication.

"Thank God," Tiffany said out loud as she wiped her tears. Envy started to think about her sister, Kema, Michael, and Mike.

"Tiffany, I can't stay here. I'm concerned about my family. I got to go. You're welcome to come with me or stay with her and wait for the police to tell them what happened."

Tiffany thought about it for a second and knew Star would be safe there, but she didn't want to be alone and wanted to clean up before she went home to her mother. "I'll come with you, Envy."

"Okay, let's go before the cops get here and we get stuck answering questions and unable to leave."

Tiffany and Envy left the hospital and jumped in the van and headed to Long Island. Envy walked into her house and was surprised that Michael wasn't home or Mike wasn't in his bed sleeping. She showed Tiffany where the bathroom was and gave her a change of fresh clothes and where the guest bedroom was. As she pulled out two guns from her dresser to feel safe, she knew there was no place safer than her house because Michael hid guns everywhere in it. She picked up the house phone and dialed Michael's number.

Michael was driving around the streets of Brooklyn. He had chopped up three drug dealers so far trying to find out from anyone that knew where his father was keeping his woman, but no one knew and this made him even more furious. The dark side he worked so hard to control was now free without the love he got from Envy and his mother. He felt there was no need to be anything else than what he was, the son of the Black Ice. He drove around looking for more victims to meet his blade, but the streets have been talking and everyone knows Evil was loose. So, all of the drug dealers shut down their business and stayed inside, then have to meet up with Evil.

Michael phone rang and he answered, "Who's this?"

"Michael, it's me baby," the voice replied.

His heart jumped. "Envy it's you. Where are you, baby? I'll kill him if he hurt you," Michael replied as tears rolled down his face and he pulled his car over.

"Michael, I'm home. I escaped. Where are you and Mike and where's my sister, baby?" Michael smiled just by knowing the fact she was safe then wondered how he was going to tell her he left Mike at the center for two days because he didn't want him to see the evil side the streets.

"Envy, I'm on my way home and then we'll talk," Michael replied.

"Okay, baby hurry up," Envy said and hung up the phone. Michael stepped on the gas and jumped on the highway home.

Black Ice's face balled up with anger as he thought about Tiffany getting away and the other women were able to get away with three duffle bags of his money. He looked at his men and wanted to kill them, but knew he only had a few left and needed them. "Fuck, I'm going to get you back bitch and teach you to never run," he yelled as his thoughts of Tiffany ran through his mind. He walked through the big steel door into the room. He looked at his hyena chained to the wall and shook his head as he realized that was the last one he had, then looked at Caesar, whose arm was chopped off from his shoulders and only had one leg left.

Caesar looked up at Black Ice standing there with a machete in his hand. His head spun from the cocaine he had been shot up with to keep him alive and not die from the pain he felt.

Black Ice raised the machete and was about to chop off Caesar's right leg. When Caesar's yelled, "Stop, stop, don't do it. I'll give you some information then will you kill me fast?"

Black Ice smiled. "Caesar, I'm not in the fucking mood to play games with you and besides nothing you can tell me can make me feel as good as to chop your leg off and watch my hyena eat it. So, you're just wasting my fucking time," Black Ice said and raised the machete.

"It's about your son and about Roxy." Black Ice stopped his attack when he heard Roxy's name. Her face came to his head. He could still see her caramel skin complexion and thick lovely body then her face was replaced by Tiffany's, who looked as if she could be Roxy's twin sister.

Black Ice grabbed Caesar by the neck and began to choke him. "You playing a foolish game and going to make me kill you even slower. There isn't shit you can tell me about my son and you want to bring up that bitch, Roxy, just makes me think of you touching her. That's why she's dead now and besides I got a new Roxy now," Black Ice yelled then released his grip.

Caesar coughed, "I'm not talking about the son you know," Caesar replied while trying to breathe.

Black Ice lifted his left eyebrow and he became curious. "Okay Caesar, tell me what the fuck you know and if it's good I'll kill you fast. No more suffering."

"Look in my back pocket. There's an envelope I found on the day Pooky and my men attacked your son and his woman. I think she dropped it and every time we attacked there was a child that has a thing for knives."

Black Ice looked at Caesar suspiciously then dug through the chains that wrapped around Caesar's body through the chair and went into his back pocket and pulled out a yellow envelope. He opened it and began to read his eyes opened wide and he smirked his devilish grin. "Thank you, Caesar, this made my night. So, my son with Roxy lived and if my son thinks I still have his woman, he'll let my blood in him take over and won't have the boy around him. So, I know where just to find him," Black Ice said out loud to himself then smiled. "Oh yeah Caesar, I lied. I'm still going to kill you slow," he yelled as he swung the machete four times chopping off Caesar's right leg. "AAHHH," Caesar's screamed in agonizing pain.

"You lie, you lie, AAHHH," Caesar screamed and cried as Black Ice picked up his leg and tossed it to the hyena across the room.

"I would love to stay and play with you, but I got some business to take care of. I'll send someone to burn your wound closed and drug you up so we can play later," Black Ice said then laughed and walked out of the room and shut the steel door.

"You fucking liar," Caesar cried as he watched the hyena once again turn one of his body parts into a mean then passed out.

Black Ice wasted no time to get ten of his henchmen ready and the five vans he had left. They took off heading towards Brownsville.

Michael pulled up in his driveway and ran into his house to find Envy sitting on the couch with Tiffany eating and talking. Envy jumped up and ran into his arms and they kissed deeply. "I thought I'd never see you again, Michael."

"Me too, baby," he replied as he used his finger to wipe her tears away. Then for the first time really looked at Tiffany, "Oh my fucking God, Tiffany," Michael said as he hugged her. My father had you too. Tiffany shook her head up and down and wanted to cry. "So, how did you get away, baby? Tiffany, tell me what happened to you and where's Star, Yasmin, and Jesse?"

Tiffany and Envy spent the next two hours telling Michael everything they had been through. Michael couldn't believe the things he heard. His father was truly a monster. Kidnapping women, raping them, and turning them into crack heads, he now understood how so many young women that came to his center got hooked to crack and when they went missing for months the things that happened to them and why they were so scared to talk. Michael told Envy everything he had did to find her and how he lost his way.

"So Michael, I'm shocked you blacked out like that, baby. You have to fight it. I always prayed I never saw it with my own eyes why the streets called you Evil, but what the fuck I can't understand is you leaving Mike in the damn community center for two days when we're all the family he has. Have you lost your fucking mind?" Envy yelled.

"I'm sorry, Envy. I wasn't thinking clearly and didn't want him to see me in the state of mind I was in."

"Fuck that, Michael. We're going to get him, now. Tiffany, come on." Envy grabbed her guns and put them in the holster and headed for the door with Michael and Tiffany following. He felt bad because he knew she was right. They hopped in the car and headed to Brooklyn.

Black Ice pulled up in front of the community center with four more vans parked up behind him. He walked to the front door followed by ten of his men. Two security guards stood there blocking the way. "Sorry, but you all can't go in there are no men allowed here. This center is for women and children," as soon as the words left the security guard's mouth, Black Ice pulled out a machete and chopped off his head in one swift move. His head went flying and rolling on the concrete. The next security guard screamed and reached for his gun as the blade of the machete stuck him in the throat and came out of the back of his neck. "Fucking, fake cops. Talk too much. Kill whoever you want, but there's a ten year old boy none of you are allowed to touch. He'll have my eyes that's how you'll know who he is when you see him. Call me or bring him into the van," Black Ice said to his men as he stepped over the guard's dead bodies and into the center.

His men followed and wasted no time to cause hell. Gunshots could be heard going off as the henchmen killed the women and security guards. Mike was on the third floor. He was laying down on one of the bed crying into a pillow. "How could he leave me and where's Envy? They forgot all about me. I knew they would. It's because of the new baby and I'm no good just the child of a crack head. That's all I'll ever be," Mike said to himself as he cried even harder and wished he was dead. Crystal walked over to his bed and rubbed his back. "Don't cry Mike. I know Michael didn't forget you. He loves you. Something must be wrong and he's trying to fix it and besides we get to spend more time together."

Mike used the pillow to wipe his tears and looked up smiling at Crystal. "That's why we are best friends, Crystal. You make me smile."

Crystal smiled back and then hugged then heard a loud noise that sounded like thunder. "What's that noise?" she asked getting scared.

Mike knew that sound all too well. "Crystal, I need you to get up under the bed and stay there something is wrong."

Crystal looked at Mike with fear in her eyes. "What about my mother, Mike?"

"Just please Crystal, do what I say."

Crystal did what Mike said and as soon as she did six henchmen dressed in black and Black Ice came upstairs to the third floor and started shooting the women and swinging machetes chopping them up. The women ran and screamed as bullets went flying everywhere and ripping through their bodies.

Mike realized he only had his switchblade on him and knew that wasn't enough to try and stop all these men from hurting everyone.

"Michael and Envy, where are you? I need you," he said out loud as he felt as if he was about to cry from watching the women begging for their lives to only be killed. They used their bodies to cover their children to protect them, but the henchmen just pulled them a part then shot them.

Black Ice smiled as he went around swinging his machete chopping off arms and legs, here and there, most of the women he had seen before and knew he had turned them into crack heads. So they were screaming, "I didn't say anything, I didn't say anything," as he chopped off a woman's foot. He saw a woman standing in a corner. He walked over to her. "Please, don't kill me. I didn't talk to anyone here, please don't hurt me."

Mike looked and could see Crystal's mother

begging for her life as a big black man stood in front of her with a gun in one hand and a machete in the next. Mike ran over toward them and pulled out his switch blade and before he could swing it into the big man's back, the man turned around and grabbed him by the neck and lifted him up in the air. Black Ice smiled as he held the boy in the air, choking him. He looked at the boy in the eyes and the knife in his hand. "It's you. I found you my boy."

"Let me go! Let me go and don't hurt Crystal's mom," Mike yelled while squirming around and trying to break free.

"Who this bitch?" Black Ice replied and raised and pointed his gun without looking and squeezed the trigger sending a bullet slamming into Crystal's mother's stomach. "AAHHH," she screamed and bent over then dropped to the floor.

"NO!" Mike yelled as he watched Crystal's mother die. He kicked and swung his feet trying to get away from Black Ice until their eyes met.

Mike stopped moving as he looked deeper into them and felt as if something was calling him and the feeling of belonging to someone. "That's right boy, don't fight me. You belong to me and it will all be clear," Black Ice stated then released his grip on Mike's neck and put him in his arms. "We're out, finish up," Black Ice yelled to his men as he headed to the van and pulled off.

Michael pulled up on the block of his community center with Envy and Tiffany in the car. The block was full of policemen and ambulances. Michael couldn't believe his eyes as he seen body bags come out of the center and was stopped by cops. "Wait! I own and run this center. What's going on here?" Michael asked as his heart filled with pain and sadness watching his life work being ripped apart.

"We know who you are sir, but you're not allowed to go in there now. A group of men came and shot up the place killing all your security guard's and staff members and some of the women even a few of the kids.

"What!" Envy yelled. "There's a boy in there named, Mike, we're his guardians."

"Miss, calm down. We'll have one of the officer's check around for him."

Envy could see one of the EMT workers carry Crystal to the back of the ambulance. Envy followed, "Crystal, where's Mike?"

Crystal was crying as the EMT worker hooked an IV into her hand.

"Miss, this girl has been shot in her shoulder and is losing blood and I believe she's still in shock."

"Crystal please, I know you can hear me. Where's Mike?"

"He tried to save my mommy and the big black man with the scar on his face killed her and took Mike," Crystal replied while crying.

"Miss, that's enough questions. I have to leave," the EMT worker said and shut the van door in Envy's face.

Michael was still in shock as Envy ran back to him. "Black Ice got him, baby. He took Mike. What are we going to do?" she said crying into his chest.

"Don't worry; we'll get him back in my heart I know Black Ice did this. I'll kill him. I swear so he can't hurt no one I love and care about anymore. We need to get away from here, Envy. I can't look at this anymore and come up with a plan to find Black Ice. You remember where you escaped from?"

Envy shook her head up and down. They hopped back into the car where Tiffany was waiting and headed back to Long Island. Inside the house, Michael pulled out three Mp5 9 mm sub- machine guns and his twin desert eagles and put them on his shoulder holsters. He saw Envy grab her twin forty caliber hand guns and a baby 9 mm. "Envy, you can't go in with me. I just want you to point it out for me and leave. I'll find my way in and bring Mike back safe."

"Michael, fuck that. I'm going in with you," Envy replied.

"Baby, you're pregnant and I'm just happy I got you back safe. Envy, I can't lose you just the thought of it makes me black out and lose control. Shit, Mike is gone because of me."

"Michael, don't say that and blame yourself. Your father is a monster and if he didn't try to hurt everyone we wouldn't be going through this. I'm going wherever the fuck you go and it's better you keep your eyes on me then you'll know I'm safe," Envy replied.

Michael shook his head up and down and handed her and Tiffany an Mp5 9 mm sub- machine gun. "Tiffany, we're going to leave you here."

"Hell no, I'm not staying anywhere by my damn self after what I've been though."

"Damn, what's with you hard headed women? I can't win for nothing," Michael said out loud making Envy and Tiffany smile.

Michael cell phone rang and he answered, "Who's this?"

"Hi my son, it's been a long time coming boy, but now you're finally ready to show your old man what you're made of."

Michael heart dropped. "You crazy fucker, what did you do with Mike and I'm not scared of you. I'm not that young boy that couldn't protect himself or my mother. I'm ready for you," Michael shouted into the phone.

Black Ice laughed. "HA HA HA HA, good boy, really good and we will see if you're all talk. Now, you fucking listen to me. I got the fucking kid and know you want him back. Your bitch helped a few of my girls get away. I want Roxy back, I mean Tiffany. I'll trade her for the boy. If I see any cops, I'll kill him very painfully. I'll call you in the fucking morning boy to meet me," Black Ice replied then hung up.

Michael stood there stuck on stupid as Envy and Tiffany watched him. "Michael, what happened? What did he say about Mike?" Envy asked with concern in her voice.

"He wants Tiffany. He told me he's willing to trade Mike for Tiffany and said there better be no cops."

"What? That means we should go tonight and get him, Michael. We can't hand Tiffany over to that monster. You have no idea what he does to women. Yes, we told you, but its different living it and have him take your body," Envy said angrily.

"I'm not going to give him Tiffany, baby, but we can't go and try to break Mike out. I know my father and he'll be expecting us. We have to come up with a better plan."

Tiffany held her head down. "I'll go back if it means he'll let a child go," she stated then began to cry.

"No Tiffany, that's not even part of the plan. I know what we're going to do. Envy, write down the address of the warehouse," Michael said. Then went and looked for a business card in his bedroom. When he found it, he dialed the number.

"Hello, Detective Roy, how are you? This is Michael."

"Oh, I see you finally called. Are you ready to turn yourself in Evil and say you killed all those drug dealers? I see someone ran up in your community center and killed a lot of people. I guess you got what you deserved."

Michael got upset the more the Detective Roy spoke. "Listen, you foolish motherfucker. Women and children got killed tonight and there's no reason to smile about that. I called your ass because I need your help. I think I know where Black Ice is and where he's holding more women. I called you before I make the call to my other police connections because I know how much you hate Black Ice. I'll give you the address, but you can't go now it has to be in the morning because he has someone that's important to me and will kill him.

So are you in or what?"

Detective Roy knew he shouldn't had laughed about the women and kids dying tonight and felt bad about it, but just hated Michael so much because he felt he was the only one who seen his true colors, but one person he hated more than Michael was Black Ice. "I'm in Michael and will get other officers down," Detective Roy replied.

"Good I'm going to make more calls and give you the address and tell you the plan so we can be ready in the morning."

Mike couldn't help, but to stare at Black Ice as he stared at him. "I see me and your mother in you boy, but let's see whose blood is stronger."

Mike looked at Black Ice and was confused. "What you mean you see my mother and yourself in me?" he asked.

Black Ice smirked his devilish grin and if it was anyone else who seen it, it would of sent chills through their body, but Mike had the same smile and cold dark eyes. "I'm your father boy. Your mother, Roxy, was my woman. I thought you died with her, but I guess you have a lot of me in you and kept on fighting. I didn't know about you until tonight."

Mike looked Black Ice in his eyes and knew he was telling the truth. He could feel it in his heart and blood that this man was his father. A father he yearned for and someone to love him. Black Ice left the room and returned dragging a woman by her hair. She screamed and cried as he tossed her in front of Mike. Mike looked at the young woman who looked to be no more than nineteen and felt bad for her. "Why are you doing this to that lady?" Mike asked.

Black Ice smacked Mike and sent him flying to the floor. "Don't ask me shit boy. You just listen. I'm going to make you into a man or even so power comes with fear. That's the only thing the world respects. Now, take that switchblade out of your pocket and kill this woman and show me what you're made of."

Mike looked at Black Ice while he rubbed his face then looked at the young lady on the floor crying. Michael's words came to his mind, 'Never hurt a woman or a girl, and treat them like God's gift to the world.' "I can't hurt her. It's wrong," Mike shouted out.

Black Ice got furious. "You've been around that ass, Michael, too long and got your mother in you. You're weak," Black Ice yelled then was about to hit him when he remembered something Caesar told him about how Mike stabbed a few of his men and Michael will kill men, but not women.

"I'm not weak," Mike shouted.

"Get up and follow me boy."

Mike got up and looked at the young lady one last time. "Thank you," she whispered. Mike smiled and followed Black Ice out of one room and then into another. As Mike entered the room, he noticed a dog like thing no kind he'd ever seen chained to a wall then a man chained to a chair. As Mike looked closer, he saw for the first time that a man's arms and legs had been chopped off.

"Now, boy prove to me that you're my son. Stab this fool up and shoot him in the head," Black

Ice ordered and passed Mike a sub- nose 38 caliber revolver. Mike took the gun and looked at Caesar and hesitated on moving.

"I see you found your next demon child the little monster looks just like you. What's taking you so long you little monster? Finish me off," Caesar said while looking at Mike.

"Boy, what's taking you so long? You want a father or what? Kill him or I'll kill you both. You're weak or are you my child?"

"I'm not weak," Mike went and stabbed Caesar in the chest repeatedly.

Caesar coughed up blood, "Yes, you little monster kill me fast," he groaned in pain.

Mike pulled the knife out of Caesar and his hand was covered in blood. He stepped back and aimed the sub-nose 38 revolver and squeezed the trigger three times. The first bullet went into Caesar's left eye and the next one into his right eye and the last one crashed into his skull and got stuck in his brain. "Just like your father," Caesar mumbled as his head dropped and he died.

Mike then walked over to the hyena and just stared at it. The hyena looked Mike in the eyes and fear took over his body then sat down. Black Ice stood there and watched and was amazed. The hyenas only feared and listened to him. Mike unchained the hyena and pointed to Caesar, "Go eat." The hyena started to laugh then ran over to Caesar and ripped big chunks of flesh off of him and ate it.

Black Ice smiled, "Yes, you are my blood boy. Now, come with me. We have to get things ready," Black Ice said while Mike walked by his side.

"Ready, for what?" Mike asked. "You'll see boy, you'll see."

Chapter 21

Detective Roy had the SWAT team surrounding the warehouse that Black Ice was in. He made sure no one could see them. Now, all he was waiting on was for Michael to get there so he could make the trade and move in.

Michael felt he could never be as ready in his life then now to face his father and finally end it. No more fear, no more worrying about his mother and loved ones will get hurt. He drove towards Brooklyn with Envy and Tiffany in the car. Envy and Tiffany checked their guns one more time as their body's shook from fear of not knowing what would happen. "You two alright? We will be there soon," Michael said.

"Yeah baby, we good, but I think you should pull over so we can pray," Envy replied.

"Yeah, you're right." Michael pulled the car over to the side of road and Envy, Michael, and Tiffany held hands.

"God please bring us out of this safe. Let your hands and love protect us out of this safely. And forgive us for any sins we may make along the way. Amen," Envy said then Michael phone rang.

He answered it, "Yeah, who is this?"

"It's me; Junior and you're heading the wrong way boy. I don't want you to go to the warehouse. Get on the FDR and head upstate," Black Ice stated.

"But, how you know which way I'm going?" Michael asked.

"Boy, I'm always watching you in some

ways," Black Ice said and the phone went dead.

"He's watching us somehow, Envy. He said to drive upstate."

"But Michael, what about the cops you have waiting at the warehouse? They can't help us if they're still watching it," Envy replied.

"You right, but now we need to move and do what he says for now," Michael replied as he started to back up the car and pulled off. He dialed Detective Roy's number.

"What the fuck is taking you so long, Michael? The SWAT team and I are ready to go."

"Detective Roy stop yelling and there's been a change of plans. Black Ice isn't in that warehouse. He knew we'd be coming. I think it's a trap and he told me to drive upstate. So, that's what I'm doing, but going to need back up," Michael replied.

"You're fucking lying. You're trying to protect that piece of shit of a father of yours. We're going in even if you're not here," Detective Roy shouted into the phone and hung up then shouted in the radio, "Move in, move in now."

The SWAT team jumped out of the truck and vans and rushed into the warehouse. "No one is keeping me away from Black Ice," Detective Roy said as he jumped out of his car and followed the SWAT team with his gun drawn. There were more than forty members of the SWAT team now in the warehouse. The first door they kicked open to find nothing in it. The next door, they found twenty women chained to a wall. "Unchain these women and get them out of here," Detective Roy ordered as he left the room. He could see four men dressed in black place something on the floor and run upstairs. "We have movement. Four suspects going up the stairs all teams move in," he yelled into the radio and followed the henchmen with the SWAT team by his side. When he got to the second floor, a henchman noticed him and the SWAT team and turned around and fired.

"Oh shit, the cops are here," a bullet crashed into one of the SWAT team members as Detective Roy dove to the ground and fired. Bullets ripped through the henchman's chest. The other four henchmen didn't have time to fire as fifteen SWAT members opened up with machine guns sending a hail of bullets ripping through their bodies. "Check the rest of the floors and keep your eyes open. There's got to be more of them here and Black Ice," Detective Roy said as he walked over to the four dead henchmen. "Hmm, I wonder what they were doing?" he said out loud to himself as he bent over and looked into a bag one of the henchmen was carrying and opened it. Detective Roy's eyes grew wide as he looked in and seen thirty digital clock bombs. "Oh shit, that's what they were doing?" he said as he realized the henchmen were setting bombs through the whole warehouse. He looked around and could see the small bombs in every corner then he looked back. The clock on them that was counting down from ten, "The place is going to blow. There's bombs everywhere," he yelled as he stood up and seen the SWAT team run for the stairs. "I'm not going to make it," Detective Roy yelled as he looked at the digital clock one more time that was counting down from two now. He seen a window and ran through it as the warehouse exploded. He fell from the second floor on top of a car as the building came down killing all of the SWAT team and women still inside. Detective Roy looked at the building go up in flames before he passed out from pain.

Michael did what Black Ice told him to and drove to a small town called, Rochester, upstate. It took him an hour and a half to get there. They pulled up in front of a house in the middle of nowhere to see Black Ice standing at the front door with a shotgun in his hand and five henchmen by his side. "Envy, Tiffany, are you two ready for this?" Michael asked.

"Yeah," Envy replied.

"No, not really, but it have to be done. I'm scared as hell," Tiffany replied.

"Don't worry, I swear, I won't leave this place until my father's dead. I want you and Envy to stay by the car if things go bad the two of you take off and don't worry about me and remember the plan. When we're about to make the trade that's when we attack," Michael stated.

"Okay, but I'm not staying by no damn car. I'm going to be by your side like a real woman, Michael," Envy replied.

"I don't have time to fight with you, Envy."

"Good then don't," Envy said as she jumped out of the car and Michael shook his head and did the same. Tiffany was the last one out. She stood by the car with the Mp5 9 mm machine gun in her hand shaking as Envy and Michael walked towards

Black Ice and his men.

"It took you long enough, boy, and I see you brought my bitch and yours as well," Black Ice said with a smirk on his face.

Michael stared. It was the first time he laid eyes on his father in years. Flashbacks of him beating his mother and him almost till death ran through his mind wildly. "I'm not scared of you and I never was and I see you're not a skinny ass crack head," Michael shouted back.

Black Ice laughed, "HA HA HA HA, you should know better Junior, you're my son. I've been waiting for you and getting myself ready for this day. It's either you be like me and help me take over everything we can get our hands on or you'll die."

"I'll never be like you," Michael shouted back as he squeezed the grip on his Mp5 9 mm tighter.

"Boy, who are you fooling? I know more about you than you do. Your first killing was that kid Razor. Who you think set that up? He works for me and was ordered to give your mother free crack. I wanted to see if you had it in you and you did and the world may not know about your little collections of body parts, but I do. Did you forget who gave you that house? There's always a way for me to get into it. Yes, my son you're just like me. So, turn over the bitch and let us cause pain to this fucking weak world together."

"I'm not like you and never will be. I'm better and where's Mike?" Michael shouted back.

"Okay, have it your way boy. There's

always another to replace you. Bring the boy out," Black Ice ordered to one of the men. The man returned with Mike by his side. Mike looked confused as he looked at Michael and Envy then Black Ice. He wanted to ask what was going on, but knew better than that. Black Ice would smack him. "Let's make the trade and get this shit over with. Bring me Tiffany," Black Ice yelled.

"No, we have them walk to us at the same time," Michael replied.

"But, I don't want to go," Mike said as he looked up at Black Ice.

"Boy, just walk and do as I say. You're not weak are you?"

Mike shook his head no and began to walk and Tiffany did the same the whole time praying in her head. Michael looked at Black Ice with hate in his eyes then looked at Envy from the corner of his eyes. Mike was now close enough for her to grab. The only problem Tiffany was just as close to Black Ice's men.

"Now," Michael screamed as he squeezed the trigger aiming at Black Ice. A hail of bullets went flying out of the machine guns. Black Ice jumped out of the way and pumped the shotgun sending bullets flying. Michael ran across the front yard while shooting. A hail of bullets ripped through one of the henchmen's face. Envy grabbed Mike by the arm and pushed him to the ground as she aimed and fired at the two henchmen running towards her. Bullets slammed into their thighs and knees making them fall face first as she aimed for their head making it explode and send brain tissue and bone fragments flying everywhere. Tiffany had pulled the gun out from behind her back when she felt a pair of arms wrap around her neck. She tried to break free as another henchman ran towards her. She squeezed the trigger sending bullets flying wild. Bullets filled the henchman's lungs and tossed him back, "Get off of me," she yelled as she still tried to break free of the man's choke hold, but had no luck. She passed out from the loss of oxygen and her body went limp.

Michael looked to see a henchman dragging Tiffany's body and aimed at his back then fired. A spray of bullets hit the henchmen in the back of his neck instantly severing his spinal cord killing him. Michael ducked behind a tree as bullets wisped pass his head.

"Evil, have you gone soft? Let's put the guns down and fight like men, boy. I know you have a machete on you, HA HA HA, you're just like me," Black Ice yelled as he ducked and continued to send shots at Michael.

"Come on Mike, we have to get Tiffany and get to the car," Envy said while trying to pull Mike and noticed all Black Ice's henchmen were dead.

"No, I don't want to go Envy. I want to stay," Mike replied while pulling away from her.

"Boy, have you lost your mind? We don't have time for this. Let's go!"

"No, I'm not going. I'm staying with my father," Envy's jaw dropped. 'Shit, he knew Black Ice is his father, but how and do he know everything. Did he know that Black Ice killed his mother?' She was about to say something when she noticed Michael dropped his gun and ripped off his shirt. Then pulled out his machete from its holster and Black Ice did the same. Both men stood there with tank tops on and machetes in their hands. You could clearly see they were related. Their muscles popping out their arms and their bodies glistened in sweat.

"Michael, don't fight him. Shoot his ass. What are you doing?" Envy yelled.

"Stay out of this, Envy. This is between me and him just get out of here," Michael shouted back as Black Ice stood one foot in front of him.

"Yeah bitch, stay out of this. This is between me and Evil here. Right boy? I know you'd fight if I called you out. I know every move you're going to make. You think I didn't know that cops would be at my warehouse in the morning?" Black Ice said then smirked. "I had my men relocate and set the place to blow. So, now every police officer that went in there is dead with about twenty crack head bitches," Black Ice said.

"Shut up," Michael yelled and swung his machete at Black Ice's head.

Black Ice blocked it with his then swung back. "You hit like your mother, boy. Show me why they call you Evil," Black Ice screamed as he swung the machete at Michael's stomach.

Michael jumped back just in time and flashbacks of his mother crying played in his head and he began to swing the machete faster and wilder. "Good boy, show me the demon in you," Black Ice said while blocking every hit. Michael spun around in a full circle and the blade cut a large piece of Black Ice's arm. Michael stopped as he seen the blood gush out. Black Ice held his arm and his face balled up with anger. "I see I need to stop playing with your ass." He kicked Michael in the stomach and began to swing the machete with all his might. Michael slumped backwards from blocking the powerful blows. "You're just like your mother weak." Michael sent an open strive and he bent low and sliced Black Ice's thigh. Black Ice hopped backwards.

"If my mother was so weak, how you get that long ass scar on your face? I'm better than you in every way, a better man and killer," Michael shouted and swung again, but missed.

Black Ice punched him in the nose making him close his eyes for a second. When he opened them, he felt the blade rip through his shoulder and stick out from the back of it. Black Ice pulled the blade out and Michael howled in pain. "You can never be a better killer than me boy," Black Ice said then swung again.

Envy watched in horror as Black Ice and Michael went blow for blow stabbing and cutting each other and didn't know what to do. She looked over at Tiffany who was still passed out and Mike who was stuck looking at the fight like her.

Michael saw another opening to strike while he was blocking Black Ice blows. He screamed and in one swift moved stuck the blade into Black Ice's stomach pushing the blade all the way through coming out of his back. Michael stood face to face with Black Ice. "I got you motherfucker."

Black Ice smiled as blood dripped out of the

side of his mouth. “I got you too, boy.”

Michael’s eyebrows rose as he looked down and could see that Black Ice had stuck him in the stomach as well and was still pushing the blade deeper in. Michael and Black Ice pulled away and stumbled backwards. Michael fell to the ground holding his stomach.

Black Ice smiled and stood over him raising the machete high. “Bye my son, you were too fucking weak.”

“No bye, asshole,” Michael shouted as he pulled out a luger 9 mm from the back of his waistband and fired two bullets that crashed into Black Ice’s chest making his body jerk and drop the machete in his hand. The next bullet slammed into his stomach and came out of his back sending him flying to the ground. Michael stood up and with one hand covering the wound on his stomach. He limped over to Black Ice and aimed the gun to his head. “I told you dad. I’m the better killer,” Michael said then smiled.

“Finish it punk, no matter what you do. You’ll always be like me and won’t be able to run from it,” Black Ice said and coughed up blood.

“I’ll make sure you stay dead this time,” Michael said and started to squeeze the trigger then a loud boom sound went off. A bullet tore through Michael’s head causing him to drop the gun. He tried to turn around to see where it came from when a bullet hit him in the shoulder, then in his rib cage, piercing his lung. He fell a few feet from Black Ice holding his rib and stomach as Mike stood over him pointing a smoking sub nose 3.8 revolver.

"I won't let you kill my father, Michael. He's all I have," Mike said pointing the gun at Michael's head.

Black Ice rolled over and smiled as blood oozed out of his wounds. "Shoot him, kill him boy, and show me you're not weak," Black Ice said as he coughed up more blood.

"I'm your bro…" Michael said, but was unable to talk and breathe at the same time.

Envy couldn't believe her eyes. Then she remembered Michael's mother's words saying how Mike would bring them great pain and he was more like his father. "No, I got to stop this," she said to herself and pulled out a baby 9 mm and stood a few feet from Mike, Michael, and Black Ice. "Mike, what are you doing? We're family. Michael loves you. I love you. Put the gun down," Envy said.

"No, you don't. You don't love me. You and Michael promised not to leave me, but you did that and left me in the community center for two days. I knew you and Michael would stop loving me once you had your own baby to love," Mike said while crying and never taking his gun out of Michael's face.

"Fuck this talking shit, boy. I'm your father and I say kill him and kill him now. Are you weak? Do you want a father or do you want to be alone?" Black Ice screamed.

Envy didn't know what to do as she looked up at Mike's facial expression. She had seen that look before on the day she first saw him stab someone up in her bathroom. She dropped to one knee and aimed her chrome baby 9 mm. "God please, don't make me do this, please don't," she prayed out loud as a tear rolled down her face. "Mike, you can't kill him. He's your brother, stop!" Envy yelled, but her words didn't reach his brain. He had blacked out and let the pain consume him. All he could hear was Black Ice's voice saying kill him or you'll be weak. He began to squeeze the trigger as a bullet ripped through the flesh of his underarm and sent him flying to the ground and knocking him out. "Oh God, oh God, please don't let him be dead, please lord," Envy said as she walked over to Mike to see that he was still breathing, but not moving. "AAHHH," she screamed because she felt so much pain. "I blame you for all of this you monster and I'm going to kill you myself," Envy shouted and turned around to aim at Black Ice, but when she looked down all she could see was Michael with his eyes open looking as if he couldn't breathe and Black Ice was nowhere to be found.

Child of a Crack Head Part 3

Two months had passed since that day; somehow on that day Envy was able to get Mike, Tiffany, and Michael in the car and drove them to the hospital. No one had seen or heard from Black Ice since. Envy and Michael walked side by side inside Harlem hospital. It took Michael a month in the hospital to heal from his wounds, but now he was feeling much better. Michael was holding a small brown teddy bear in his hand. "You think he'll wake up today," Envy asked and wanted to cry.

"Yes baby, if he don't wake up today, then very soon. I can feel it."

Ever since Envy shot Mike that day to keep him from killing Michael, he has been in a coma and hasn't woke up since. Every day Michael and Envy visited him and prayed that he'd wake up. Michael forgave Mike for shooting him. He knew that it was because of Black Ice pushing him and the fact Mike just wanted to belong and have a family something he never had. As they walked down the hall, Michael noticed a woman with a big bag and a church hat on her head that looked like Janet. "No that can be her," he said to himself as he and Envy opened Mike's room door and the surprise of their life. Black Ice stood over Mike's head rubbing his head. He turned his head to see Envy and Michael standing at the door way and smiled his devilish grin. Then pulled out his 44 bulldog revolver from his waist at the same time Envy and Michael opened their jackets and pulled their guns out of their holsters. All three of them stood there with their guns aimed……